FINDING
REFUGE

ISBN: 978-1-960810-96-0
Finding Refuge

Copyright © 2024 by David Rollins
All rights reserved.

This is a work of historical fiction. As such, the appearance of certain historical figures and instances are inevitable. All other characters, businesses, places, events, and incidents in this book are the product of the author's imagination. Any resemblance to actual persons, living or dead, or actual events is purely coincidental.

No part of this publication may be reproduced, distributed, or transmitted in any form or by any means, including photocopying, recording, or other electronic or mechanical methods, without the prior written permission of the publisher, except in the case of brief quotations embodied in critical reviews and certain other noncommercial uses permitted by copyright law.

For permission requests, write to the publisher at the address below.

Yorkshire Publishing
2488 E 81st St.
Ste 2000
Tulsa, OK 74137
www.YorkshirePublishing.com
918.394.2665

Published in the USA

FINDING REFUGE

David Rollins

DEDICATION

For my friend, Al Esquer

ACKNOWLEDGMENTS

To Al and Daniele Esquer and Dana and Laurie Schoening for your inspiration and friendship.

To Robert "Grif" Griffith for your friendship and mentorship.

All my love to my wife Kim, my daughter Kaitlyn, and my son Nathan for their patience, love, and understanding of my desire to write.

Thank you, God, for this wonderful variable in my life.

PREFACE

The American bison, or buffalo, once numbered in the millions throughout North America. During the 1870s, the buffalo population diminished to mere hundreds. Except for small herds scattered across the Great Plains, this icon of the American West began to dwindle. Soon, the buffalo were on the brink of extinction. By 1876, they were nearly gone.

Efforts were made to save the buffalo. Focus was placed on how to restore their numbers. Protective actions were initiated to provide land, or sanctuaries, where the buffalo could live without harm. Some of these sanctuaries later became national parks, game preserves, and wildlife refuges. Many are still thriving today, such as Yellowstone National Park in Wyoming and the Wichita Mountains Wildlife Refuge in Oklahoma.

It took time to establish the success of these sanctuaries. Various obstacles, such as challenges in legislation, funding, and land acquisition, required significant work to overcome. Support organizations formed to help create animal sanctuaries to save various species. While risks to buffalo safety remained, the collective efforts of many agencies and organizations helped minimize concerns. Threats to buffalo survival ranged from poaching to tick-borne illness. The success of the sanctuaries was vital for buffalo stability.

As the buffalo population increased, other wildlife became susceptible to risk. The hunting of predators, such as bears and mountain lions, led to a significant reduction in numbers. To ensure the protection of buffalo sanctuaries, some predators were eradicated. Prevention measures were utilized to safeguard buffalo breeding from predators that would harm the calves.

For many predator species, some prevention measures meant removal or extermination without regard for their survival. These unfortunate animals were driven from their native lands or forced to acclimate in remote areas. While history tells of buffalo tribulations and how these animals overcame adversity, other wildlife suffered. Some predator species had no escape and no refuge.

Few predators endured this more than the American wolf.

PROLOGUE

October 1907

A young Comanche girl sat on her grandfather's lap. He swayed the front porch rocking chair in slow intervals back and forth. The comforting motion kept rhythm with her metered narration. Kiyiya spoke softly in Comanche, pleased to have his precious granddaughter develop an appreciation for their treasured dialect. He soothed the frustration of her creative mind and offered a reprieve for her literary endeavor. Proud of her intellectual level as an elementary school student, he encouraged her promising talent.

Mayuri gripped her writing pad and pencil with a mild temper. The motivation to write the greatest poem ever was subdued by the daunting task of creating a title. Her little hands pounded on the writing pad as she scribbled through another attempt. Kiyiya held her hands. He whispered through her long, braided hair and calmed her contentious mind. Confident of her attention, he leaned her against his chest and continued pace with the rocking chair.

"I have a story for you," he said quietly in Comanche. "A story that began long ago and is still happening today as we sit together. It is a story that wants to be told, but it is waiting for an ending."

"How can a story not have an ending?" she asked.

"All stories have endings, but this one is waiting for you to write it."

"But I want to write a poem! One that we can read together and sing together," she said.

"I know," Kiyiya replied. "But this story can give you an idea for your poem. And then you can think of a title."

She reluctantly agreed. "Okay, Grandfather. What is your story about?"

Satisfied with her curiosity, he put her writing pad and pencil on the porch and placed his aged hands over her tiny palms. He squeezed her with a loving hug and cleared his throat. With the gentle sway of the rocking chair, he led her back through time.

"From the Wichita Mountains here in Oklahoma Territory many years ago, a young boy, about your age, looked across the land from a hilltop. He waited for the sun to rise so he could see. As the light became day, he watched for the buffalo to come. There were so many buffalo, they covered the ground. You could not see the grass. Their hooves made the sound of thunder before a storm. The ground rumbled, and the dust swirled. The boy watched them pass until the sun was high. There were so many buffalo, he could not see them all. As the boy grew up, the buffalo became less. One day, when the boy was a man, he went to watch for the buffalo again. But the buffalo did not come back."

"Where did they go?" Mayuri asked.

"He did not know. So he looked for the buffalo. He went to faraway places. But still, the buffalo did not come back. He was sad, for he missed the buffalo. He hoped that one day, the buffalo would return to the Wichita Mountains. Even today, he still hopes for their return."

"That boy was you, wasn't it?" she asked.

"Maybe," Kiyiya joked.

She gave him a joyous hug. "When will the buffalo come back?" she asked.

"I don't know. But that will be the ending to the story. That is what you are waiting to write about," Kiyiya said. "Maybe that can be your poem?"

"That story is sad," she replied.

"Yes, it is. But maybe you can write a happy ending someday."

"And I still need a title." She thought for a moment and looked up at Kiyiya. "Grandfather, what about your secret? Is that part of your story too?"

"My secret?"

"You know! Your gift with wolves."

Kiyiya chuckled. "That is *our* secret. No one else is to know," he said and tickled her side. She laughed as he continued. "What about it?"

"When we visit the Wichita Mountains and see the wolves, they are like the buffalo in your story."

Kiyiya stopped the rocking chair. "What do you mean?"

"There are not many wolves in the mountains anymore. Are the wolves going away too?" she asked.

Kiyiya hesitated at her observant question. He contemplated an answer as he stared into her attentive brown eyes. Sadness began to overcome him, as he was unable to think of an encouraging response. Wiping a tear from his face, he held her close and looked at the horizon.

"I don't know," he said.

CHAPTER 1

March 1872

The horses trudged through the deep snow. They heaved against the burdensome drifts, which buried them to the stirrups. The biting cold stiffened their strides as they angled up the ridge. Their riders nudged them through the lodgepole pines in futile efforts to find the trail. The rising elevation thinned the chilling air as the horses breathed harder with every stride. The cirrus clouds intensified with varying shades of amber and pink. The rising glow cast a brightening array of violet and blue across the white-capped mountain peaks. The frigid night awakened to another wintry morn without reprieve.

"This is far enough. The horses need to rest."

"They are just on the other side of this rise."

Two men urged their weary mounts to the top of the ridge. They dismounted with snowshoes and trudged through the drifts. The numerous pines with snow-covered branches impeded their forward movement. Every step required more depth to each breath as they navigated the forest. One man pointed to a clearing ahead. Having traversed thirty yards or less, they continued to the opening in the trees.

"There!" one man shouted.

The other man gasped for air with his hands on his knees. The sight was stunning.

A river wove through the snowbanks with a deep-blue hue emanating with each ripple of the current. A vast field stretched into the remoteness, limited by the adjacent tree line and bordering mountain ranges. The snow-covered pines outlined the majestic scene. Several trails zigzagged through the drifts, exposing the prints of predators in search of morning meals.

"By the river. Opposite bank. There they are."

Both men saw a line of giant brown beasts lumbering along the riverside. They pushed through the snow near the water's edge with minimal effort. Their shaggy brown presence created a stark contrast against the pillowy, white landscape around them. The steady formation and determined effort accentuated the natural beauty of the display.

"You were right, John. This place is amazing. And look at those buffalo!" The man paused to enjoy the panorama. "We have done well."

"This is everything we worked for and hoped it would be. And now we are finally here. Congratulations, Andrew!"

"Don't congratulate me! That goes entirely to you. Without your determination, we would still be panhandling away in some committee back East."

"Obtaining this land is just the beginning, Andrew. With this amount of acreage and it being so remote, we can implement the next phase of our plan."

"Whoa now, I don't think we need to get ahead of ourselves. Let's enjoy the moment before it's gone. You know how long it took us to simply achieve this."

John walked to the center of the opening. "Every day we wait is another day lost. This land is ready. Now we can stock it."

Andrew watched an eagle glide overhead. "Securing a park this large against poachers and hunters will be challenging. I wouldn't even know where to begin incorporating that into a bill for legislation, let alone finance it. This part of the country is still the Wild West in many regards."

"We have no choice," John replied. "Politics will have to handle any security for now. With the next phase, we gather what animals we can and work on how to get them here."

"The buffalo?" Andrew asked. "John, you know everyone back East wants the buffalo gone. The executive branch wants it more than any of them. The whole thing is a political agenda stretching from the legislative to the military. I suggest we pick our battles with the least resistance. And that is not saying much, considering the rumors that abound about the slaughter taking place on the Great Plains."

John continued watching the buffalo follow the riverbank. The small herd strolled in unison. He watched the scene with reverence. His mind struggled with the process to pursue the demands before him, while his heart felt the moment that was to determine both fate and history. "And that is exactly why we continue with our agenda."

"It will be difficult to hide this. We need President Grant to continue—"

"We aren't hiding anything!" John said. "Grant got the credit he wanted for creating the first national park. And here it is. My only hope is that there are many more national parks to come. Anything else regarding Grant or any politician is on a need-to-know basis. I am proud of what you are trying to do in Washington. Everyone involved with this endeavor knows we need you there. But until this can become fully realized, there must be limitations on those not vested in our work. This is too fragile to become a pawn for political gain. Or worse, sabotage."

"We need the politicians," Andrew responded. "We cannot further our agenda without their influence. I can help with that. Once I am elected as a representative, our voice will be heard."

"I know you will do well. And I do not say that based upon the pretense that you are my son-in-law. Rebecca is proud of you too."

Andrew grinned in satisfaction.

"But you forget the influence of our financial power. It is that power that will help put you in office and continue to fuel our momentum in creating more parks across the country." John paused. "It is the passage of time that is becoming our greatest adversary—and the adversary of the wild animals being hunted to near extinction with each moment. That is what this park is for and why its purpose must continue to be achieved."

"Exactly!" Andrew said with scorn. "We hide it." He looked across the valley and spotted a small pack of wolves running near the tree line. "And what is this you said about many more parks to come? Are you going rogue on us?"

"Do not be naive. Like I said, this is only the beginning. The government cannot protect the future of this country's wildlife with the urgency that it needs. We must act now."

"By hiding wildlife in national parks?" Andrew asked.

"By saving it on lands created for sanctuary. What those lands are identified as does not matter. I don't care if you name them parks, preserves, zoos, or territorial places of refuge. Call them whatever you want. It's only our plan that matters."

"That is a large task. Even with the financial and political influences, how do we secure such an endeavor a thousand miles away?" Andrew asked.

"We continue to better organize and increase our membership. Our next strength will be our numbers. And until we can get the right person of position to lead us, we need to scatter our members throughout the country. Just like the army, we must send scouts along every trail and into every territory. We reduce the distance between areas of concern with dedicated local observation. We string a line of trusted representatives for communication to provide accurate reports so we can better manage our time. The extended weakness of the politicians trying to manage this chaos from the East is failing." John continued to vent. "We need to get back to Washington and arrange a meeting with the other members. We must tell them it is time."

Andrew watched the line of buffalo meander away. "At the rate the buffalo are being killed, this could get concerning in the years to come."

"The influx of treaties and changing regulations will continue to bog down the legislators and hopefully confine the hunting to limited areas. It will buy us some time, but it will not last. The real threats are those we cannot control and have no awareness of. They will hasten the problem and make it worse. And not only for the buffalo," John replied.

"The buffalo are the only threatened species."

John noticed the wolves approaching the river behind the buffalo. "No, there will be others." A revitalized expression warmed John's chilled face. "I'm glad we came out here. Come on. The horses are rested. We need to get back."

Andrew high-stepped through the snow, trying to stay in his previous tracks. "You know, I like what you said earlier about sending scouts along trails to every territory. It has a ring to it. Our fledgling society does not have an official name yet, does it?"

"Not one that has been agreed upon."

"Well then. When I get elected to Congress, I'll make that my first decree." Andrew raised his arm in the air. "By proclamation, I hereby ordain the inauguration of the prestigious and ever-so-clandestine Trails to Territories Society!"

Both men laughed as they steadied their horses.

Bam!

Both horses reared upward in surprise, throwing John and Andrew into the snow.

Andrew hurried to his feet, exclaiming, "That was a gunshot!"

John wiped his face and surveyed the area. "And it was close."

Bam! Bam!

"That way!" Andrew yelled. He calmed his horse and mounted the saddle. His eyes widened with concern. "Oh no, the buffalo! Surely, no one is stupid enough to hunt in a national park."

"They gave away their position by firing more than once. I'd say stupid is rather certain at this point. Get to the top of the ridge, but stay hidden."

They churned through the snow and angled to the summit. Careful to stay among the trees, they reached a draw that provided a camouflaged view of the valley. Three men on horseback bounded through the snow along the riverbank. John and Andrew watched as they circled several objects in the snow.

"What are those?" Andrew asked.

"Wolves," John responded. "They shot the entire pack. They were after the buffalo herd."

Andrew became angry as the three men waited near the river. He watched as the buffalo herd ran toward the three men. "What are those buffalo doing? They turned around."

John looked ahead. "There, behind the buffalo."

They watched as three more men on horseback drove the buffalo herd up the riverbank. The mighty animals barreled through the snow. A fine mist rose behind them, creating a cloud of crystals that glistened in the rising sunlight. The herd bunched together in the deepening snow, trapped between the river and the horsemen. The three men in front of the approaching herd dismounted and formed a line. John and Andrew watched as the men took a knee and opened fire.

"No!" Andrew yelled.

Several buffalo fell in front, causing confusion among the trailing herd. The animals gathered around the dead leaders. The three men following opened fire from their steady positions, dropping more of the helpless animals. The accuracy of the cross fire and precision of the ambush dwindled the buffalo herd in seconds. Only the remaining smaller animals were spared as they scattered across the dense snow.

"Andrew, get back!" John yelled.

"Look what they are doing! They've nearly killed them all. What is the point of a national park if this is going to happen right in front of us!"

"They don't know we are here. And this has only recently been deemed a national park, so I doubt any hunter knows that, let alone is willing to obey it. Now, come on. There is nothing we can do," John said. "They are after the buffalo's winter hides."

Andrew nudged his horse and galloped into the open at the top of the ridge. He led his horse down the embankment and onto a level clearing leading to the valley. He watched the hunters gather around their kills as two of them waved at Andrew. He brought his horse to a rapid stop, then stood in the stirrups.

"They aren't waving at you." Andrew whipped around as four men emerged from the brush, carrying rifles. He saw two wagons hidden in the trees behind them. Several fires simmered in seclusion. The men gradually surrounded Andrew.

Andrew engaged them. "Gentlemen, this land is now known as the Yellowstone National Park. Those buffalo are within the park boundaries. I recommend you stop immediately and—"

Bam!

Andrew's horse reared and sprinted away from the men. Andrew held on to the reins as John waved frantically at him to catch up. Both men urged their mounts through the snowdrifts. Shots continued to explode behind them. They leaned low in their saddles, desperate to reach the other side of the summit. The pine branches

Finding Refuge

tore at their faces as they charged through the forest. The gunshots became muffled as Andrew and John evaded the hunters.

"Let the horses rest for a minute!" John yelled. He swatted several pine needles and snow from his face. "What were you thinking, getting that close?"

An odd silence alerted his attention. He looked over at Andrew's horse and saw it wandering with an empty saddle. John panicked and urged his mount toward the trees. He searched underneath the branches for Andrew. He motioned his horse to advance and raced along the previous tracks. He dodged the trees while tugging on the reins to navigate the trail. A thick pine grove blocked his advance as he moved away from the dense branches. A large mass hung from one of the limbs. He stopped his horse and noticed legs dangling above the snow.

"Andrew!" John directed his horse underneath the branch and pulled at Andrew's coat. Andrew moaned and fell backward into the snow. John leapt from his saddle and rolled Andrew face up. A red swath stained the snow. "Where are you hit?"

Through the blood oozing from his forehead, Andrew mumbled, "I'm cold."

"You stay with me. I've got to get you to your mount. Can you get up?"

Andrew winced through the pain and reached for John's shoulder. "Tell Becky . . . I . . ."

John brushed the blood from his mouth. "Andrew!" He held him tightly as the steam from his breath ceased. Anguish overwhelmed him as he embraced Andrew. Checking his vitals a final time, he laid him gently in the snow.

A distant whistle distracted him. He got up and bounded toward the sound. He found himself back at the location of the shooting. He wiped his eyes to see the wagons hurrying along the riverbank.

Several mounted men escorted the wagons with rifles drawn, urging the horses forward.

John noticed red-and-white buffalo carcasses strewn across the valley. Huge blood stains appeared as small pools against the bright whiteness of the snow. The hunters' efficiency amazed him. They'd skinned each kill in minimal time. The wagons, burdened with fresh winter hides, tongues, and buffalo heads, left deep ruts as they rushed away. One buffalo was skinned in the river, leaving a stream of blood flowing along the bank. The ghastly sight, combined with Andrew's death, overcame John. He fell to his knees, sobbing, as the hunters fled.

June 1874

The summer wind swayed through the prairie grasses, appearing as waves across the Kansas countryside. The occasional rise of a hill provided the only terrain feature in the barren vastness. The Great Plains offered a view of land and sky that met beyond the horizon. The cloudless blue and sprawling emerald accentuated the arrival of summer with the warm breeze. The expanse of the view created a sense of isolation for the timid and boundless tranquility for the bold.

In a prone position, John Bruce peered through the grasses along the rise. After many months of acquaintance with the seemingly endless plains, he could not fully acclimate after being in the Rocky Mountains. The rising heat and constant wind proved alien to the comfort and elevation of the Rockies. His appreciation for the sight of a dense forest became a yearning he'd never realized before. A snow-capped mountain was difficult to envision as he looked across the green hills and open fields.

A herd of buffalo grazed nearby. Their dark coats in shades of tan and brown blended with the tall wheat-colored grasses of the plains. They strolled through the area, portraying a presence of belonging to the land. John tried to imagine the numerous herds of folklore that had dominated the West by the millions. The sparse number before him led to questions of concern. He hadn't known what to expect from his first venture into the buffalo range of Kansas, and the sense of disappointment was not his preference.

"I remember there being more of them," Trey Doyle said. He shielded the sun from his face. "I scouted this area twice before you arrived. There were easily a couple hundred here a few days ago. I asked some buffalo hunters to make sure. They all suggested the fields surrounding these hills."

"I am surprised hunters would offer their hunting grounds to just anyone," John said.

"That's true. But there is nothing that a little convincing and some bribery cannot solve. Your money bought this view today. I hope what few buffalo are down there meet some of your expectations."

"Maybe they broke away from the main herd?" John asked. "I would love to see a huge mass of them on the move."

"It's possible. This area is known for large seasonal migrations. It has also been rumored to be nearly hunted out. Any herds spotted here are separated or being killed off. I'm afraid this is it. I know that is not what you wanted to hear."

"How far do the hunters go onto the plains to find them? Are there any other areas nearby where the buffalo are plentiful?" John asked.

Trey came to a knee and pointed farther west. "We would need more supplies, but if we kept heading west toward Colorado Territory, many of the larger outfits hunt there. It is all a matter of where they can find them and how high their quotas are. Some outfits—"

Bam!

John and Trey dove for the ground as the piercing sound of a gunshot exploded from the adjacent hill. They flattened in the prairie grass and looked in the direction of the gunfire. Several more shots came from other positions. The largest buffalo fell first. The herd stumbled around in confusion. Each shot found a target as the buffalo dropped one at a time. The remaining buffalo pawed at the ground as multiple shots joined in unison. The sound vibrated across the plains in a thunderous wake. John and Trey watched the buffalo diminish in rapid succession.

The guns fired for ten minutes or more. The thriving herd of nearly one hundred buffalo dwindled to half that. Spurred by the devastation, a surviving buffalo charged ahead, encouraging the remaining herd to follow. Shots continued to erupt as escaping buffalo submitted to the steady stream of fifty-caliber bullets. Several buffalo staggered from stray shots that slowed their run, ultimately succumbing to the assault.

Random gunshots finished off any wounded buffalo as the area became quiet. John and Trey watched the field. A quick count of the carnage revealed forty-five buffalo dead. The grisly scene depicted deceased buffalo strewn across the field. The remaining survivors formed a desperate line of escape and sprinted for the open plains.

The silence seemed fitting as the wind whistled its return. It moved through the area as a haunting whisper from the spirits of the departed.

Trey stood for a better view. "Get down!" John said and pulled him to the ground. "I thought you said you are a scout."

"I am," Trey replied and yanked his arm from John's grasp. "I can be a scout, a hunter, and anything else money can buy."

"I lost someone doing what you just did," John said. "Stay low. Next, they will go down and inspect their kills." Both men watched as four horsemen galloped after the fleeing herd. Five more descended on horseback, riding among the dead buffalo. Two of the men waved toward the hill. "They are signaling the skinners. Watch."

Four wagons rushed to the killing field. They circled the dead buffalo and parked. Several more men jumped from the wagons and hurried to the nearest animal. Some of the men wore long drapes tied around their waists. Each unsheathed various knives and went to work. The mounted men kept their guns drawn and yelled at the workers tending to the buffalo. The horsemen motivated the workers by shouting orders and yelling at other men to prepare the wagons. They worked at a relentless pace. The seasoned experience and efficiency of their work impressed John and Trey as they observed the entire operation.

Within a few hours, the hides were stripped from every animal. The carcasses lay bare across the ground. Blood saturated the earth, turning the grass into the color of tar. Random buffalo heads were taken, adding to the gruesome devastation. The men worked in teams, hauling the hides to a wagon and packing them in bundles. The wagon creaked from the weight of the skins and heads. A few of the horsemen waved at the remaining wagons to follow.

The remaining wagon lumbered up the hill. The stacks of hides were visible against the wooden rails. Two men drove the wagon while one man covered the rear, holding a rifle at the ready. The horses gathered speed as the driver steered them eastward across the prairie. John and Trey determined their destination and watched the vultures descend upon the rotting carcasses.

Both men stood. The view below resembled a war zone. The ground was carved by wheel ruts that appeared like scars across the grass. Lifeless bodies littered the area. The senseless killing had manifested into a graveyard of death that neglected the honor of burial. The sheer waste of potential sustenance imposed a shameful tragedy against nature. The scene of the slaughtered beasts and former rulers of the plains bore a terrible glimpse into the future of their demise.

"That was the most organized work I've ever seen," Trey said. "Most hunting parties take a whole day to do what they did in a few hours. And it sounds like they are finishing off the rest of the herd. That will be a heck of a payday when they go to settle."

"Is that what this is to you? A payday?" John asked. He continued staring at the dead buffalo. "We have been tracking these hunters for months now. After seeing this, I am convinced they are killing the buffalo by the thousands per week."

"More like by the tens of thousands. This was one hunting party that did all of this in two hours. There are hundreds of parties out there doing this every day. You may not like money as much as another, but can you imagine how much they are making off those hides at the rate we just saw?"

John ignored him. "I didn't know it was this bad. To see this level of carnage in only two years? Our estimates were wrong. This is much worse." He sighed with grief. "I've seen enough. I need to report to the society right away."

"We've gone much farther than our planned route. It will be a while before we find a town. You want to look for the army? That column we saw yesterday can't be too far away," Trey said.

"The army doesn't care about what's happening here, and the society doesn't want them involved. I need to send a telegram. Where's the closest town?"

Trey took a last look at the bloody carcasses as the vultures circled above. "I think you are too late, Mr. Bruce. No one can stop this killing, not even your society. If you want my opinion, I say we would be better off profiting from this. Everyone else is. I mean, look around. What else is there to do in a place like this?"

"Profiting from the killing of buffalo is what we are trying to prevent, Mr. Doyle. We are paying you to scout and report, nothing else."

"So, it's Mr. Doyle now, huh? Well, either way, it's just a thought. Besides, those hunters have this so well organized, it's practically its own trade. Perhaps you and your society could save the buffalo by regulating hunting. You could limit the number of hunters, charge some fees here and there, and make enough money to fund your whole operation."

"It's obvious you were not at Yellowstone when hunters just like them killed my son-in-law. They don't care about regulations, Mr. Doyle. Look around you! Does anything you see lead you to think that some limit is the answer? By the time the government takes any action, there will only be the scattered bones of what was once the American buffalo," John replied.

"Again, just a thought. We hide in the grass with nothing to show for it while those hunters get rich. What is there to save?"

John hurried to his horse and mounted. He stared at Trey with rising bitterness. "I'm betting that wagon of hides is headed to a town. I'm going to follow them and see where they go. I may try to see how many more outfits are coming in to sell."

"I hope you can count because everyone out here is looking to sell except us," Trey replied. He sneered at John from underneath his cowboy hat.

John angled his horse in the direction of the departed wagon. "Mr. Doyle, you are welcome to follow. Once we get to the next town, you draw the wages I owe you. Your services are no longer required."

"You've had enough of this, huh?"

John spurred his horse. "I've had enough of you."

CHAPTER 2

June 1874

The old wagon wheels creaked from extended use as the tired team slowed to a trot. Dust swirled behind the burdened rig. The steady passing of horses and wagons compacted the busy thoroughfare of Front Street. Wooden buildings lined the dirt road, with the block lettering of outfitters, a mercantile, and a fair share of saloons. An eighteen-year-old man wiped the sweat from his brow. The relentless heat ravaged his thirst. He slapped the dust from his soiled cowboy hat and looked at the town with distaste. The noise and bustle already made him miss the tranquility of the Great Plains. He stopped the horses and set the brake.

"This is it?" Noah Wrath asked.

"Yes! Contain your excitement," Fernando Raul replied. "Dodge City." He stood from the wagon seat and stretched. "Back to civilization. Our journey is over. Come on. You move like an old man."

"You are six years older than me, Fern," Noah replied.

"All the more reason you should be six steps ahead. Look around. Tonight, it's white sheets, a warm bath, and a meal we didn't have to shoot and skin," Fern said. "Ah, the thought of fine eating that can only be found farther south. We are so close." Fernando reminisced about the savory cuisine of his Mexican heritage.

He dismounted the wagon. Every business flourished with customers eager for transactions. He strolled alongside the walkway for a closer view of the buildings. "There!" he yelled at Noah. "Let's try that one."

Noah followed Fern to the nearest mercantile. They entered the building and removed their cowboy hats, happy to be free of the blistering sun. A man stepped from a back room while yelling orders to others in the shop. Several men moved hastily, loading a wagon with barrels and various supplies.

"What can I do for you boys?" the man asked from behind the counter.

"Fernando Raul," Fern stated and extended his hand. "This is Noah Wrath. We would like to—"

"Buffalo hunters, am I right?" the man asked.

Fern continued. "—sell you some top-quality hides. They are winter coats, thick and heavy. And yes, we are professional hunters. Also for hire."

"Looking for another contract?" The man jeered. "I'm Ellis Hamilton, proprietor. How many skins do you have?"

"It's a lighter load this trip. But, like I said, the quality of the hides will more than make up for the number," Fern replied.

"Buffalo getting scarce, huh?" Ellis asked. "I've been hearing that from quite a few of you hunters. Western Kansas has seen better days. The larger herds are getting tougher to find, and when they are, it takes days to get back and find a buyer. Where's your wagon?"

Fern pointed out the window.

Ellis yelled at his clerk, "Go inspect those hides and get me an estimate!" He looked at Fern. "I pay a fair price, but only if they are what you say they are. I'm tired of these thin summer coats they keep bringing in here and expecting winter coat payouts. Darn fools. You all should know to hunt buffalo in the winter."

"Our load is late for the season. But our hides are what I say they are. You won't be disappointed," Fern said. "About the summer hides, did you happen to hear where any of the larger herds are gathering in these parts?"

"Like I said, it's getting harder to find them. Herds are smaller, and they scatter. There are hundreds of you hunters out there shooting up every buffalo you can find."

Fern leaned on the counter. "My friend and I are looking for work. We are a two-man operation and provide good hides with a quick return. You contract with us, and we can meet your supply need at a steady rate."

Ellis opened a ledger and made some notes. "I'm not looking for any contracts. Besides, you are not going to find enough buffalo with a two-man outfit to meet Dodge City quotas. Most of the larger operations are pushing farther north and west. They are bringing the big numbers for big orders." Ellis paused from his accounting. "To compete for contracts around here, you two should start looking where you shouldn't. It's the only way you have a chance for any real business."

Noah noticed his friend's growing impatience. Fern was the negotiator and salesman between the two of them. His understanding of people and terse business savvy were seasoned skills he employed with every buyer. But the long journey to Dodge City had tired him. Noah became entertained watching Fern wrestle with his depleting tolerance for Ellis.

"We do not hunt on treaty lands, Mr. Hamilton, if that is what you are referring to," Fern said.

"Why not? Are you two partisans? Abiding by shallow rules with some blind loyalty? All they do is change the treaties each time the wind blows and expand the hunting grounds even farther. What is illegal today is wide open tomorrow. Money moves the line," Ellis responded.

"That may be, Mr. Hamilton, but we don't want any trouble with Indians or the army," Fern replied. "Do you know of any contracts at all? We need the work."

"No. The smaller outfits can't handle the demand."

The clerk handed Ellis a paper. Ellis reviewed the writing and agreed to buy the hides from Fern and Noah. They exchanged funds, and the hunters began to leave.

Then the clerk whispered at Ellis. Ellis slammed his ledger on the counter and stomped toward the door. Fern and Noah watched as Ellis argued with the clerk. With an angry bearing, he directed the clerk back outside. Ellis rubbed his head and realized Fern and Noah were still standing in the store. He exhaled and recovered from his tirade.

"Well, gentlemen. It seems I have a complication in one of my business ventures. However, it can offer us an opportunity that can be mutually beneficial." Ellis looked out the window at his wagon. "I am short a hand that is needed for a supply run to an encampment in Texas. As I am over a barrel here, I need to get those wagons moving within the hour. You said you are looking for work? I could sure use one of you to ride escort. And as it is short notice, I'll pay triple the rate plus expenses. But I need an answer now."

Noah peered at Fern and cleared his throat. Fern ignored him and addressed Ellis. "That sounds good, Mr. Hamilton. For us anyway. Where is this wagon train going to in Texas? As you know, there's a whole lotta Texas out there."

"It's a small camp near the old Adobe Walls. It's not far. We should be back in no time with your help," Ellis said.

Noah stepped in front of Fern. "That's Indian Territory."

"It's a resupply. We deliver the goods and turn around that day," Ellis replied. "If there are any buffalo hunters passing through while we are there, maybe you can ask them where the buffalo are. It's an opportunity, and you're getting paid to find your next hunt."

Noah watched Fern, expecting a reply. Fern led Noah outside, "If you don't mind, Mr. Hamilton, we would like to discuss this."

"If one of you is standing by those wagons when I come out, I'll take that as a yes," Ellis said.

Fern and Noah walked to their empty wagon and sat on the tailgate. Noah leaned against the side wall and propped his leg up. "We need the money, and it sounds simple enough. I'll go."

"Are you sure about this? We don't know anything about this guy. And you are still going into Indian Territory."

"For what he is paying, I think we can afford the risk."

"Not if it means getting killed! I know you prefer living on the plains your whole life, away from every living soul. But this isn't some buffalo hunt where the shooting is one-sided. This time, they can shoot back," Fern said.

"I can handle myself. This is nothing."

Fern stared at Noah, concerned by his friend's demeanor. "I don't know how many men are going on this trip, but remember, they are people. And where there are people—"

"There are problems," Noah answered and rolled his eyes at Fern.

"Don't lose your temper if things get crazy out there."

Noah nudged Fern with his boot. "You get us another hunt, and I won't have to lose my temper."

"I should have left you where I found you. You're nothing but trouble."

"Then you would have no one to shoot buffalo for you. With your aim, you'd starve to death," Noah said.

"I taught you everything, youngster. Don't forget that." Fern climbed off the wagon. "All right. It's settled. I'll look for work while you're gone." Fern pondered as he stared down the street. "He did have a point about asking any hunters about the buffalo herds. If you happen to get the chance, ask around. But not if they are on treaty lands. We want no part of that. Do you hear me?"

Noah jumped off the wagon and approached the mercantile. "You enjoy that bath and those white sheets tonight, Mr. Raul. And stay away from the poker tables. You can't bluff to save your life!"

"You just make sure you save yours." Fern mumbled an uneasy prayer as he watched Noah wave without looking back.

The wagons rolled over the Great Plains grasses in a determined effort to reach their destination. Ellis Hamilton kept the wagon train moving without tiring the horses. Nights passed quickly, and the wagons stopped only when it was too dark to see the terrain. Men slept between watches. The wheels were moving the moment the sky displayed a hint of sunlight. The resupply effort felt more like a race for the men than a job.

The landscape was vast. Their route from the plains of Kansas, through No Man's Land, and across upper Texas provided a grand scene of earth and sky. The view appeared endless in all directions. The summer heat and scorching sun gave the travelers a constant thirst. The two wagons carried three men each, with Ellis and another man on horseback. Noah rode in the back of the trailing wagon. He kept away from the other men and enjoyed the peace of the open prairie. The plains offered him a sense of contentment, freeing his mind from the harbors of the past and the uncertainties of the present. The passing panorama provided him with a feeling of home.

Noah saw the few contours of the area. Landmarks and vegetation were scarce. The use of direction was the only trusted guide available for the journey. A slope rose from a wash along their route. They traversed the minor depression to spare extra effort on the horses.

Noah felt the sun on his face as he tried to stay awake through the rumble of the wagon. He wiped his face and noticed a pair of ears protruding from the brush along the top of the ridge. He squinted to see the snout and distinct features of a gray wolf prone in the grass. It watched the passing wagons with patient curiosity.

One of the men whistled at the horses. The wolf stood, eager with interest. Noah noticed the blending shades of tan, gray, and white in the animal's fur. Its silhouette exhibited untamed strength and the potential for speed. The predator commanded a majestic presence as it stared down at the foreign travelers. One of the drivers cracked the reins. The wolf shifted its position for a better view.

"Hey, look up yonder!" a man riding in the front wagon yelled. Noah watched the wolf remain intent upon the scene below it.

Bam!

A shot rang out, jolting Noah. He looked at the front wagon. Two men aimed their rifles at the wolf. They fired in unison, missing each time. Another man on horseback fired his revolver at the wolf, causing a ricochet that kicked up a small cloud of dust next to it. The animal jumped from the impact and continued watching the wagons.

"Quit firing!" Noah shouted at the men. "Leave it alone!"

Both wagons stopped. The men from each wagon lowered their rifles and stared at Noah. One man propped his rifle stock on top of the seat back and leaned against the barrel, facing Noah.

"What did you say?" the man asked.

Noah looked at him and loosened his revolver from the holster. He came to a knee and balanced against the side wall. "Leave the wolf alone. You are drawing attention to our location."

"Since when do you tell us what to do, boy?" the man yelled.

Noah gritted his teeth. His eyes met the man's with a menacing glare. "Don't."

"And now you think you can bark orders?" He placed his hand on the heel of his revolver.

With striking speed, Noah pulled his revolver and fired. The shot splintered the man's rifle stock. His weight shifted from leaning on the rifle, then he slammed into the seat and collapsed onto the ground. The other men looked back at Noah, who had his revolver already back in the holster.

"What is going on back here? Who is firing?" Ellis asked as he rode up from his lead position.

The men remained silent.

The other man got up and dusted himself off. He grabbed his hat and looked at Noah. "That fool shot at me!"

"It sounds like a battle over here. You fired all those shots?"

Noah watched the men as they remained still. He waited a few seconds and then placed his hand over his holster.

"Answer!" Ellis shouted.

One man nervously responded, "No, sir. There was this wolf up yonder there in the grass, and that young fella told us to stop shooting. Then he shot Lloyd's rifle out from under him and—"

"Shut up!" Ellis yelled. He looked at each man and then watched Noah sit down. "Adobe Walls is close. With all that racket you made, we will lie low and rest the horses for the night. I plan to get there early in the morning. Anyone else who fires without permission will deal with me!"

The men scurried to refresh the horses and secure the wagons. Noah walked up the ridge. He reached the top and witnessed a plateau near a valley with a possible water source. The wind soothed his temper and calmed his demeanor. Disdain clouded his thoughts as he felt regret for taking the job. He wanted to keep walking and lose himself in the solitude of the plains.

He looked east and stopped. An Indian sat motionless on horseback, staring at him. Movement caught Noah's attention as a wolf bounded toward him. It ran with full strides, growling upon approach. Noah placed his hand on his revolver. He stared at the wolf, intent to make eye contact with the attacking predator before drawing his weapon. A strange sense consumed his presence as the wolf made eye contact with him. The animal shortened its leaps and shuffled to a stop a few feet in front of Noah.

The wolf growled its contempt, keeping its eyes fixed on Noah. Noah breathed heavily, unsure of what to do. The wolf stalked Noah. Compelled beyond his own reason, Noah reached out for the wolf. The animal stood four feet high, and its sleek torso was longer in length. Its distinctive nose and tan eyes completed the revered features of the Great Plains hunter.

A moment ensued as they moved closer to each other. The wolf sniffed Noah's boot and pant leg. Noah knelt and extended his hand. The wolf gathered his scent and again made eye contact. Noah stroked the fur behind its ear. The initial contact was met with caution, but the encounter continued. Noah rubbed the wolf's head. The animal calmed, turning as if to indicate a prime spot for Noah's attention.

The Indian shouted a terse call. The wolf's ears flared upward. Without notice, it streaked at the mounted Indian. Noah remained on one knee, watching the wolf depart. He saw the Indian stay still. He was too far away for Noah to distinguish him. The wolf circled the Indian and stopped next to him. Noah admired the sight before him. The Indian, sitting proudly on his horse on the grass-covered plains, was an enduring portrait with the unique presence of the gray wolf.

"Interesting."

Noah stood to see Ellis watching behind him on horseback. Ellis frowned his displeasure at the sight of the Indian. "I guess the men weren't lying after all." He pulled his rifle from the casing. "Get out of the way." He aimed at the Indian.

Noah drew his revolver and aimed at Ellis. "Don't."

Ellis kept his aim upon the Indian. "I said move!"

Noah cocked the hammer.

Ellis lowered his rifle. "You are an odd sort, boy. Get back to the wagon. I don't tolerate deserters, and I won't hesitate to—"

"I'm not your boy. And don't threaten me again. With the idiots you have on this drive, I'd make quick work of all of you."

Noah sent a menacing glare at Ellis. His daring words and fearless presence pierced Ellis with sudden uneasiness. The unexpected challenge to his authority caught him off guard. He witnessed Noah's sinister expression and deduced that the young man was no stranger to confrontation. What began to scare him was not the threat of confrontation but that Noah appeared to welcome it. Struggling to conceal his fractured ego, Ellis cased his rifle and rode back to the wagons.

Noah looked back at the Indian, who remained with the wolf near his side. Then a moment passed as the Indian directed his mount over the distant ridge. Noah continued to observe the vacant view. He walked back to the wagons, unaware of the hundreds of Indians gathered in the next valley.

As Noah approached the wagon, several of the men encircled him. His temper overcame him as the men continued to position themselves while yelling taunts and threats. He drew his revolver and fired multiple shots near their feet. Two men ran. The remaining two raised their rifles at Noah. Noah targeted their chests and prepared to fire.

"Stop!" Ellis shouted from his mount.

One man standing by the wagon fired at the ground near Noah. Noah watched the dirt scatter from the impact. He looked at Ellis, noticing the uncertainty on his face. Without warning, Noah pulled his knife from the sheath and spun around. He flung the knife next to the man, burying the blade into the wooden wagon.

The man jumped away from the knife as Noah drew his revolver and fired along both sides of him. The bullets slammed into the wagon. The man dropped his weapon and fell to his knees, raising his hands in the air.

Noah holstered his revolver and approached the man. He yanked his knife from the wood and pointed the blade at the man. "Don't think that I missed. Either time."

"Enough!" Ellis yelled. "Get to the wagons. All of you, watch for Indians. Keep your guns drawn. There won't be much sleep tonight. Expect an early morning. We aren't stopping until we reach Adobe Walls!" Ellis continued shouting orders at the men and then addressed Noah. "Be glad you can shoot, or I would leave you out here."

Noah tapped on the heel of his revolver.

Ellis leaned closer to him and said, "When we finish this run, I never want to see you again." He spurred his horse and rode to the front of the wagons.

The sun pierced the horizon with welcome light. The group's predawn rise gained them two hours of travel time. Navigating the darkness proved challenging in the limited moonlight. Ellis continued motivating the wagon train forward. The weary men scouted the route for hidden obstacles. The team steered around a small butte and found numerous ruts along the ground. Ellis directed them ahead. The men cheered at the sight of the dwellings.

The encampment was small, with few amenities and structures. A sparse number of people inhabited the desolate location. The feeble attempt to recover the meager town from its demise years earlier had been motivated by wandering buffalo hunters and desperate entrepreneurs. Ellis guided the wagons behind a sod structure and directed the men. They unhitched the arriving wagons and quickly guided the horse teams to covered wagons parked nearby.

Noah stepped aside. He watched the men work frantically to hitch the teams and ready the covered wagons for departure. The men's fevered effort and the constant prodding from Ellis sparked his curiosity. A man ran from the sod building and approached Ellis, who handed the man a leather pouch. The rustle of several clinking coins sounded from the bag. Ellis tipped his cowboy hat at the man and rallied the group.

Noah stepped through the commotion. He unfastened a corner and lifted the tarp. Numerous bales of thick buffalo hides were packed tightly in the wagon. The weight of the hides settled the wheels firmly on the ground. The hides were stacked three bales high, with other skins piled neatly on top. He was astonished at the prized merchandise. He checked the next wagon and saw more hides waiting for transport.

"Get a mount. You are riding horseback to Dodge City. Keep your gun drawn and guard my wagons," Ellis said to him.

"I thought we were hauling supplies," Noah said. "These hides are fresh—a few days at most. You aren't allowed to hunt here."

"Like I said, you have to go where the buffalo are. Mount up."

Noah backed away. "I don't want any part of this."

Ellis pulled his gun and aimed at Noah. "I've had enough of you. You get a mount, load your saddlebags, and get moving, or you can forfeit your pay and stay here."

A man yelled from the front of the building. "Look!" He pointed anxiously at the nearest ridge. "They're coming!"

Hundreds of mounted Indians crested the ridge. The staggered line of horses stretched along the grassy contour of the slope. Guns and spears protruded from their grasps at the ready. The warriors and their horses were adorned with tribal accents of earth-toned paints and rustic articles alluding to battle.

Noah watched the massing assault with trepidation. He grabbed a saddled horse and evaded the scrambling people. A peculiar moment overcame him. He paused in the surrounding bedlam as intrigue consumed his spirit. He witnessed the alarming view again. A subtle peace calmed his mind while he observed the scene. The native plainsmen sat upon their mounts with the rising sun at their backs. He saw the living portrait in timeless splendor. If only for an instant, Noah knew he was witnessing history.

"Get these wagons out of here!" Ellis yelled. "Ride north. Find any terrain you can for cover, but keep moving."

The wagon teams sprinted away, with riders leading the way forward. Noah spurred his horse to a full gallop away from the encampment. He looked back to see the charge take place. Gunfire echoed throughout the area. Whoops and chants became louder as Noah motivated his horse for more speed. A ravine leading northeast appeared through the grass. He rode for the depth of the washout. Noah took a final glance at the encampment. Clouds of dust from swarming mounts filled the air as gunfire erupted without pause. He entered the ravine and continued away from the battle.

Bam!

Noah's horse reared violently from the noise, throwing him onto the hard ground. Noah groaned and grabbed his back. He rolled over and witnessed his horse stagger awkwardly and fall. A trail of blood oozed from its side. Noah struggled to gain his awareness. He crawled to his dead mount and braced against it to stand. He rubbed his eyes and saw Ellis on the other side of the washout.

Bam!

Ellis fired his rifle at Noah, kicking up dirt next to him. He aimed and fired again as Noah dropped for cover behind his dead horse. The round impacted in his saddle. Noah reached for his revolver. He looked down to see an empty holster. Panic ensued. He wiped his face and noticed blood across his glove. He peered over the saddle. Ellis steadied for another shot.

Bam!

Noah shuddered as a gunshot exploded from the embankment behind him. He looked at the rim of the ravine, unable to see from the angle of the bright sunlight. He checked his distance from Ellis. Noah watched his horse rear angrily upward. Ellis pulled the reins while pressing his hand against his bloody right leg. He regained control of his flailing mount and spurred its sides. Then he took off across the washout and disappeared over the opposite bank.

Noah sat for a moment. He listened for the sounds of anyone nearby. He checked his head and regained his composure. He crawled up the embankment and peered over the rim. A gray wolf stared directly in his face. It growled a threatening warning and showed its teeth. Noah froze and surrendered any notion of action.

A horse whinnied from the top of the embankment. Noah shielded his eyes to see a mounted Indian staring down at him. The Indian called to the wolf. The predator backed away from Noah, giving him a better view of the animal. Noah recognized the wolf and realized it was the Indian he'd seen before. The wolf stepped closer toward Noah, unable to contain its curiosity, and sniffed him. Noah extended his hand carefully and looked into the wolf's eyes. He rubbed behind its ears and head as the wolf nudged him in satisfaction.

The Indian watched with amazement. He spoke to the wolf again. It reluctantly returned to his side and sat. Noah stood to see the Indian.

He was dressed in various leathers that appeared different from what the Indians Noah had witnessed at the encampment had worn. Nothing about the Indian appeared aggressive in nature. He portrayed a stoic presence. He watched Noah with a combination of curiosity and wisdom. The Indian looked around and directed his horse down the embankment. Noah followed as the wolf eagerly took the opportunity to reengage with Noah.

The Indian and Noah stared at each other without words. Noah guessed the man to be older but fully capable of challenging him. He pondered what tribe the man belonged to. The language barrier limited their interaction. Noah determined the man to be someone of position. The portrayal of wisdom reminded him of Fernando. The comforting thought eased his tension as he yearned to know the man before him.

A minute passed as Noah became weary. His head pounded in pain from the injury. He wiped more blood from his brow. He watched the Indian, still unsure what to do. The wolf playfully bit at Noah's leg. Without expression, the Indian pulled an arrow from a quiver. Noah became uneasy. The Indian looked at Noah and then at the wolf. He spoke in his language. Noah remained still, watching with a sense of reverence and hoping not to provoke any misunderstanding.

The Indian moved his arm in a sweeping motion and broke the arrow in half. He extended his hand to Noah. Noah approached him and held out his own hand. The Indian placed an arrowhead on Noah's palm. He spoke in his language again and pointed at the wolf and then at Noah.

The Indian nodded at Noah with a sense of completion. Confused, Noah bowed in return, keeping eye contact with the Indian to ensure a respectful intent. The wolf pawed at Noah, then stopped. Its ears perked as its eyes became sharp and attentive. It raced up the embankment. Noah followed and looked over the rim. Several Indians on horseback were riding toward them.

"Whoa," Noah mumbled.

The Indian rode in front of Noah to the top of the embankment. He waved at the approaching group. They stopped their advance and waited. The Indian looked at Noah. A sense of understanding seemed to emanate between them. Noah watched the Indian gallop away. The wolf acknowledged Noah for the final time, then hurried after its master.

Noah watched the Indian greet the group. He heard some speech echo through the wind but was unable to understand it. The group joined together and rode away.

Noah watched them depart. The experience overwhelmed him. The unique sense of connection with the Indian and the wolf was something he had never felt before. His soul yearned for more while his mind raced for reason. The unexpected feeling of joy puzzled him. He yearned to find a purpose for the event and understand why his life had been spared. Through it all, he felt contentment, knowing that his life had just changed.

Noah stumbled to his fallen mount. He emptied the saddlebags and took what he could carry, then grabbed his canteen. His head still hurt from the injury. Fatigue began to overcome him as he leaned against the saddle. He pulled the strap of his rifle case and tied it into a sling.

The area became quiet. The wind tossed the grass along the edge of the embankment. He slid down the saddle and sat on a hard object buried in the dirt. He brushed the earth away, revealing his lost revolver. He held the weapon with relief and stretched his legs across the ground.

Finding a comfortable position with his back against the saddle, he reached in his pocket and held the arrowhead. The chiseled flint appeared large against his palm. It spanned three inches in length and was an inch and a half wide at the base. Numerous ridges lined the piece from precise impacts that had formed a razor-sharp edge on both sides. The tip was carved to perfection and was thick enough to penetrate the toughest hides.

He holstered his revolver and held the arrowhead in the sunlight. The shaped rock was his reminder of a moment he had never expected but now greatly cherished. He lowered his arm and rubbed his thumb across the rough surface of the arrowhead. He thought of the Indian and the wolf, recalling each moment of the encounter. He clenched the arrowhead with fondness. The warm air beckoned his weariness. He lowered his head against the soft saddlebag and suddenly felt compelled to say a few words.

"Thank you." He glanced at the sky with reverence and then surrendered to sleep in the passing breeze.

CHAPTER 3

June 1874

Noah splashed cool water across his face and filled his canteen. The stream flowed with fresh water from a recent thunderstorm. He had navigated the stream across the barren terrain, using the water to replenish his strength and hunting game along its banks. The horizon flickered with lightning and the prolonged echo of distant thunder. The wind kept up a steady rate, providing welcome relief from the heat of the day. As it was one of the few streams angling eastward, Noah followed it for direction and sustenance.

The sun reached its zenith as he trekked through his third day on the plains. Land stretched for miles with nothing to see but the wilds of nature. The stream and the timing of the thunderstorm eased his concerns for basic survival. Uncertain of a more northerly approach and not wanting to abandon what the stream provided, he continued along its winding path.

A valley came within sight. The subtle south-central plateaus outlined the basin with sloping boundaries.

Noah noticed the widening stream. Small pools formed in the lower areas of the valley. A gathering of dark objects caught his attention. He shielded his eyes to see a small herd of grazing buffalo. His instinct engaged. He watched eagerly to determine the direction of the herd, locate any terrain features for an advantage, and then identify the lead buffalo. He visualized aiming his rifle to kill the lead bull, causing the herd to gather in confusion long enough for him to select his next targets.

He saw the grazing herd and cleared his mind. The lead bull's head, with its blunt, curved horns and muscular neck, swayed up and down from feeding. Its summer coat exhibited earth tones of tan and brown that blended with the sage-colored grasses.

The herd moved in unison. The picturesque scene resonated within Noah. As he watched the majestic animals meander across the land, he began to appreciate them. For years, he had seen the buffalo as the means to an end. All he knew was the relentless demand of the hunt, the determined kill, and the constant pursuit of a payoff. The obsessive work that the buffalo represented obstructed any view of simplicity. For the first time, he abandoned his persistent past and appreciated the serene spectacle before him.

He proceeded along the bank and quickened his steps to maximize the daylight. His legs ached from the journey, adding to the pain of his head injury. He jumped over a rock and heard the distinct rumble of buffalo hooves. He peered ahead to see the herd stampede. The animals raced together across the stream. Noah noticed a lone horseman calling out behind the buffalo. The rider slowed his mount and watched the buffalo disperse. Then he turned his horse around and trotted away.

Noah looked ahead of the horseman. Thousands of longhorn cattle migrated through the valley. The herd stretched over the rise and wandered in a wide column. Several riders guided the herd. Wagons pursued the herd over the rugged terrain. Noah was amazed at the sight of the massive cattle drive.

"Hey there!"

Noah spun around. An older man sat atop his mount, clothed in the garb of a seasoned cattleman. His sweat-stained cowboy hat, bandanna, flannel shirt, leather vest, and worn chaps accentuated his coarse voice. The man rode toward Noah, sitting high in the saddle and exposing a revolver on each hip. He stopped near Noah and offered a hearty welcome.

"Did you lose your mount?" the man asked.

"Yes, sir. About three days ago," Noah replied.

"Three days? Goodness, that is no way to travel out here, son. Open prairie without a mount is a surefire way to death. If the plains don't get ya, the Indians will."

"I agree. I've had a bit of both," Noah said. He extended his hand. "I'm Noah Wrath."

"Jerill Oren. I own a spread near Fredericksburg, Texas, northwest of San Antonio. We're taking a herd up the Western Trail."

"This is the Western?" Noah asked.

"Yep. We're bound for Dodge City."

Noah rubbed his head. "I didn't realize I went so far east. Are we still in Texas?"

"You're in No Man's Land. Indian Territory. Where are you coming from?" Jerill asked.

"Near Adobe Walls. I was on a wagon train running supplies to an encampment there."

"Adobe Walls! Is that where you were three days ago?"

"Yes, sir. We had a run-in with some Indians."

Jerill laughed. "A run-in? Over five hundred Comanches attacked that place, from what I hear! Word's been spreading all over the plains. We've been driving the herd all day and some of the night when we can. I'm hoping to get to Dodge City without any trouble. Did you escape from Adobe Walls?"

"I guess you could say that," Noah said. "It happened fast. I lost my horse riding out of there. I've been on foot ever since."

"Where are you trying to get to?"

"Same place you are. I was headed back to Dodge City when they attacked." Noah paused. "Did you say they were Comanches?"

Jerill nodded.

Noah thought of the Indian and the wolf. He felt fulfillment in knowing the mysterious man's tribal background.

"That's my outfit down yonder. I've got some good boys working for me. You're welcome to join us. Dodge City isn't much farther, and I can always use an extra hand to bring in the herd. I pay a fair wage if you can handle a mount and keep my cows moving forward," Jerill said.

"That's the best offer I've had in a while. Thank you, Mr. Oren," Noah responded.

"I'll have one of my hands get you a mount and saddle. I see you are no stranger to a six-shooter and a long gun."

"I've hunted my share of buffalo."

"Buffalo hunter, eh? It's a good trade, but there won't be much calling for buffalo soon. They are getting fewer by the day. Longhorns are the mainstay now," Jerill stated. He watched his passing herd with pride.

"I can't argue that." Noah shifted his gear and wiped his forehead. Fatigue began to weaken him.

"When's the last time you had something to eat?" Jerill asked.

"I could use a good meal," Noah said.

Jerill directed him to the wagons. "That second team is my Cookie. He's a German settler and one of the finest chefs I've ever known. He makes the best meals this side of Deutschland. We eat like kings for a cattle drive. He will be setting up soon. Go see him for a plate and some water."

"I'm much obliged, Mr. Oren."

The sun settled behind the horizon, marking the stopping point for the drive. Jerill Oren summoned his cowhands around the chuck wagon to meet Noah. The men appeared to be near his age. They welcomed him with ample food and spirited stories of the drive. Noah was bombarded with questions about his ordeal at Adobe Walls. Every man quizzed him on his experience there, eager to hear of the event that was expanding in popularity.

Noah told stories of his buffalo encounters and life on the Great Plains. The cowhands were fascinated by the many locations Noah had visited across the prairie country. Their numerous questions about the Rocky Mountains, Indian encounters, and the vast buffalo herds amazed Noah. He chuckled at the slight German accent some of the men had. They gave Noah a warm welcome and expressed a feeling of home and family that he had not experienced in years. The cowboys joked in unison, with Jerill as their cherished instigator. The day's hard work and demands vanished in celebration of food and friendship. Noah embraced the unique group's contagious spirit with sincere appreciation.

Many of the young men knew only life on the ranch and working longhorns for Jerill. Noah noticed that they revered Jerill as a father figure. Each man referred to him as sir—not as an employer but as a person of stature. He performed his role as trail boss with respect and mentorship. The men seemed to thirst for his attention and guidance. Noah noticed undertones of loyalty and devotion that resonated deeply from each man. Noah shared his experiences with them, considering his stories as mere work and survival. But the more he spoke, the more he realized the men considered his experiences as adventures.

The evening meal ended with each man negotiating his order for night watch. Cookie surprised the gathering with a Dutch oven full of warm cobbler. The aroma of simmering glazed peaches under a moist, caramelized crust enticed the men without effort. They rushed to form a line with bowls and spoons as if preparing for battle. The men scarfed the dessert down and licked their bowls clean. They finished the evening chores for Cookie and then rested their bellies with gluttonous satisfaction.

"Noah, what did you think of that meal?" Jerill asked.

"The best I've ever had on the prairie, Mr. Oren," Noah replied. "I may never leave."

"Yes, indeed." Jerill praised his cook. "That was some fine Texas hospitality, Cookie. We are all indebted to you for another great meal." Jerill stood in the center of the men. "Well, boys. Another day without injury or mishap and a fine meal to see its end. And we have been blessed with a visitor to aid in our journey. Noah, welcome. Now, if you all have your shifts for the night, let's join together."

Noah watched the men bow their heads. He waited for something to happen, unsure of what he should do. A few seconds passed before Jerill led a prayer. Noah was stunned at the group's expectation of the humble act. In all his time on the plains, he had never witnessed such unified devotion. Cookie removed his hat and joined in the moment. Noah bowed his head and listened to Jerill's words. He prayed for the day, the safety of the men, and their loved ones back in Texas.

Jerill gave reverence to blessings received from another day of life. He continued to listen as Jerill mentioned Noah in his prayer. He gave thanks for Noah's safe arrival and asked for blessings upon his journey. Jerill concluded his prayer with each man saying a hearty "Amen" in unison.

Noah watched the group disperse and prepare for the night. The sense of joy that abounded from the group mesmerized him. The men carried out their duties with a peacefulness that he had never seen before. Two of them mounted and prepared for their night shift. Jerill sent them off with encouragement and their orders. Several of the men bedded down for sleep before their shift arrived. Noah arranged his belongings and unrolled his bedding.

Cookie lit his oil lantern and set it on the ground. He reached under the wagon for the breakfast storage crate to prepare for morning. Unable to locate the handle, he moved his lantern farther under the wagon. The light illuminated the ground as he crawled headfirst toward the crate.

"Ah!" Cookie yelled as the lantern cast its glow across a five-foot-long diamondback rattlesnake slithering under the wagon. The serpent angled its head and coiled within striking range of Cookie's face.

Bam! Bam! Bam!

Three gunshots shattered the evening stillness with deafening percussions. Jerill and several of the men pulled Cookie out from underneath the wagon. Cookie leaned against the front wheel and hyperventilated from the terrifying experience. Two men tried to calm him as Jerill searched for the rattlesnake. He held his revolver forward and moved the lantern under the wagon. The snake flopped in two pieces, with half its head blown away. Jerill grabbed a cooking knife and sliced the remaining part of the head off the body. Two of the men dragged the snake away and buried the head.

"Cookie, did it bite you?" Jerill asked frantically as he held the lantern up and searched Cookie's face and hands.

"I don't think so. I don't feel any pain, other than being scared half to death."

Jerill patted Cookie's shoulder in relief. He stood to survey the encampment. "Who fired those shots?"

Noah reloaded his revolver. "I did. Is Cookie all right?"

"Hold on a moment. You fired those shots from over there? You're thirty feet from the wagon."

Noah replaced his revolver in the holster and approached Cookie. Relieved Cookie was not bitten, he faced Jerill, who was still standing in amazement. "I heard the rattle. I figured I could give Cookie a better chance at getting away before it struck at him."

"You blew its head off with three shots from thirty feet away!" Jerill exclaimed.

"I know. I wanted to be sure I got it. I would have done it in two if it weren't so dark."

The group gazed at Noah. Jerill addressed Noah with continued wonder. "I've never seen anything like that in my life. You have quite a talent, Noah. Thank you for saving Cookie. That could have been very bad."

The other men congratulated Noah with praises and envious questions. Jerill ended the event by directing everyone to their bedrolls for the night. He watched Noah sort his belongings and bed down. Turning to check on Cookie, he whispered a grateful prayer.

"Thank you for sparing Cookie tonight, Lord. And for sending us that talented young man."

Morning arrived with the holler of the lead cowhand. The men were positioned along either side of the herd, beckoning the mighty beasts forward. The calls between the cattle echoed across the valley. The giant formation appeared as a rolling wave of horns and hides over the land. The longhorns lumbered ahead, finding their direction with instinct. Jerill admired the western scene from the ridge. He watched his men get underway and start another day on the Great Western Trail.

Jerill spoke to Cookie as he tidied from breakfast and packed the wagon. They acknowledged their comments with Jerill pointing northwest. Cookie gave him a confident salute as Jerill rode ahead to find Noah. The herd strolled forward. Jerill navigated to each man, relaying orders and checking their well-being. He completed his rounds and galloped alongside Noah.

"Noah, how would you like to put your buffalo hunter skills to use and ride ahead with me to scout for Dodge City? I could use a good tracker to keep me going in the right direction."

"Scouting was my friend's job. I mostly pulled the trigger. But I can keep you company if we both get lost."

"That's the spirit!" Jerill said.

They motivated their horses and sprinted ahead of the herd. The valley opened to the wide expanse of the plains. Noah began to recognize the vastness of Kansas, leaving any terrain features behind them. They slowed their mounts to a canter and angled ahead. The barren landscape left little for observation as Jerill filled the void with welcome discussion.

"Tell me, Noah. Where in the world did you learn to shoot like that? That was nothing short of amazing, what you did last night. You saved Cookie's life."

"Lots of practice. I have a friend who taught me a few things. Mostly how to aim and shoot, but also how to feel it. It may sound awkward, but I guess it comes natural to me."

"Interesting. It obviously works for you." Jerill looked Noah in the eyes. "I hope it doesn't cause any ill will between us, but I have to ask, son. Are you a gunman?"

"No, sir. I don't have any trouble with the law, if that's what you mean."

"I didn't mean to imply any law trouble. I've just never seen anyone with the skills you have handling a gun who wasn't a gunman."

"I've pulled a lot of triggers," Noah replied.

"I hope you didn't pull them at anything with two legs," Jerill stated. They rode for a few moments before Jerill continued. "I'm surprised you haven't asked me about the men yet. I'm sure you must have a curiosity by now."

"I know your men have high regard for you. But I guess with you and Cookie being the older men on the drive, that is to be expected."

"Old! I'll take that as a compliment, I guess." They both chuckled. "I hire Cookie for all our drives. He's a good man, and trust is hard to find. But the boys are mine. Not by birth, though. My wife and I run an orphanage back home. This is how we put food on the table and hopefully, with God's strength, help nurture a few young souls along the way."

"All of those men are orphans?" Noah asked.

"You may refer to them as men, but they are all your age or younger. They are young men to me. And they all have promise."

Noah faced Jerill with hesitation and then surrendered to the moment. "You're a preacher, aren't you?"

"Most of my life. I'm a parson for a small congregation. Ranchers and their families attend. Fine folks from Germany, Mexico, and several from back East. My wife and I came out to Texas as missionaries many years ago. We settled down, and before we knew it, we had a church. Very blessed. But, if you live long enough, tragedy finds you. Sickness struck many of our number, leaving some children without parents. Other children were orphans from ghastly situations of all kinds. You name it. So, my wife and I decided to do something about it. We got into cattle to help with costs and food. It proved to be helpful. The boys gained confidence working a ranch, and the girls learned various trades and skills. My wife is a teacher and educates each child. We couldn't be prouder of them."

Noah listened intently to Jerill. He looked ahead as memories collided with the man's narrative. "And you think I'm amazing for shooting a gun. You are the one who is amazing. You have a heart. Those young men should be grateful. I know I would be."

Jerill let his words resonate before addressing Noah. "So, what is a bold young man like you doing way out here on the Great Plains? And I don't mean having survived the Comanches attacking some camp at Adobe Walls."

"Just trying to make a living."

"Trying to make a living or trying to find a life?" Jerill asked. He focused on Noah with emphasis on his question. "The two are very different for someone your age."

"You see things in people, don't you?" Noah asked.

"I've been around, son. Long enough to know a good thing when I see one. But also to know when I see someone in need."

"Not to taunt you, but what exactly do you think I need? You don't even know me."

Jerill did not hesitate with his response. "A purpose."

Noah stopped his horse. He stared at Jerill with unbridled wonder. "How did you . . ." The subtle words caught Noah off guard. His eyes welled with tears. He wiped his eyes and gained his composure. Tired of reservation and concern for his words, he spoke with genuineness. "Mr. Oren, this may sound odd, but are you an angel?"

"Son, I am just a man. A man trying to make a difference and serve the Lord where I can. And, when the opportunity presents, inspire a few souls."

"You have certainly done that."

They continued their journey northwest, while watching the sun angle toward the horizon. Noah explored a small slope, hoping to gain a vantage point for an extended view. He reached elevation and looked ahead. Smoke from several structures twisted in the wind. Wagon trains from east and west formed lines leading to the same destination. Noah signaled Jerill to join him.

"There it is. Dodge City," Noah said.

"Well done. It is closer than I thought. I think the men and I will enjoy knowing this is our last night under the stars for a few days. We will bring the herd in tomorrow and hope for a good night's stay in one of those hotels before heading back."

"That is a fast turnaround. Why so soon?" Noah asked.

"Family. How about you? You mentioned your friend might be here."

"I don't know. A lot has happened since I left him for the wagon train to Adobe Walls. I'll have to see if he is still here," Noah said.

"Then get started. Go find your friend."

"What? What about the herd? And this is your horse. I can't pay you for—"

"It is my gift to you," Jerill said. "The saddle too. It is the least I can do after you saved Cookie's life." Jerill extended his hand. "You find your friend. But if your situation changes, you know where to find us. God bless you, son."

"Thank you, Mr. Oren."

Jerill tipped his cowboy hat at Noah. "God has a purpose for you. Don't give up on Him."

Noah concealed his sorrow over Jerill's unexpected departure as the man galloped away to find the herd.

Noah directed his mount along the dirt street. He approached the same mercantile and tied his horse at the front of the building. He searched the road for anyone resembling Fernando. The town bustled with steady traffic, appearing to have more activity than when he departed for Adobe Walls. Seeing no potential of locating Fernando, Noah faced the mercantile. He readied his revolver in anticipation of meeting Ellis Hamilton again.

"How can I help you?" the same clerk asked as Noah approached the counter. "Wait. I remember you. You went on that supply run to Adobe Walls with Mr. Hamilton. Is he with you?"

"What are you talking about?" Noah asked.

The clerk rushed to the window. "Where are the wagons? Did he go around back?"

"I'm alone. Is Hamilton not here?"

"No. I figured he might be with you." The clerk became discouraged and returned to his place behind the counter.

"We got split up. I don't know where he is." Noah questioned the disappointed clerk. "I'm looking for my friend, Fernando Raul. He was with me before I left for Adobe Walls. Have you seen him around town?"

"I remember him too. From what I recall, he tried to go after you. He said something about a new contract he got, then left to bring you back to Dodge City. I have not seen him since then. From what I hear, he probably got to Adobe Walls when the Comanche attacked," the clerk stated. "We have not heard from anyone at Adobe Walls yet."

"How long ago did he leave? I'm going after him," Noah said.

"You can't! There is war in that area now. The army is keeping everyone from going south. That's why the town has gotten so crowded. Folks are scared to venture out too far. I'm sorry about your friend."

Noah turned toward the door. "He's not dead. He's much too smart for that."

"All right. I warned you. But if you decide to go, could you do me a favor? I'm not sure what to tell him, but if you see Mr. Hamilton—"

Noah swung around with his revolver in hand. *Bam!* He fired at the center of a mirror behind the clerk. The heavy glass fractured into numerous cracks that resembled a giant spider web. The clerk, who'd ducked, peeked over the edge of the counter. The whites of his eyes were visible from the door as Noah holstered his revolver.

"Now you have something to tell him," Noah said. He flung the door open and walked to the edge of the street.

People passed in every direction. A few nearby had heard the shot but went about their business. He despised the congested scene. The steady crowd and surrounding buildings made him feel trapped.

He felt boxed in and watched the disarray with bitter contempt. The thought of Fernando missing or gone filled him with uneasiness. Standing among the crowd, Noah felt alone as he struggled for direction.

He thought of Jerill Oren. The sense of belonging called to him. He yearned for the peacefulness of the open prairie and the duty of the cattle drive. Without Fernando to guide the way forward, he was lost. He approached his horse, conceding to escape the town and find Jerill.

Then he heard a voice behind him. "Excuse me, young man."

Noah saw two army cavalrymen on horseback. He recognized the rank of one as captain. A sergeant waited behind him.

"How old are you?" the captain asked.

"Old enough."

"There is no need to be ornery about it. It's a simple question," the captain said.

"Eighteen," Noah replied.

"That's what I thought." The captain sat back in his saddle. "We are looking for strong men, like yourself, to join the army. I'm sure you've heard what happened at Adobe Walls." Noah remained silent. "Anyway, we are mustering all the men we can find. What do you say you follow us over to recruitment?"

Noah reached into his pocket and retrieved the arrowhead. He rubbed the jagged flint and thought of the encounter with fondness. "I'm not interested, Captain."

"I just told you that your country needs soldiers to fight. You would be fulfilling an obligation. Besides, it is also steady employment, which I'm sure you could use," the captain said. "Sergeant, escort this man to headquarters."

Then another voice came from behind Noah.

"He is already employed with the army. Leave him alone."

Noah recognized the familiar voice. "Fern!"

Noah and Fern welcomed each other with a firm embrace.

"It's good to see you," Noah said.

"It's good to see you alive. When I heard about Adobe Walls, I thought for sure you were dead." Fern grasped Noah by his shoulders. He expressed relief over Noah's return. "I've been checking the mercantile for any word. No one came back. Unless someone came with you, I think you are the only one to return from the supply train."

The captain moved his horse between Noah and Fern and said, "Sergeant, escort this man." He then addressed Fern. "What's your story?"

"This man and I are contracted to drive cattle and supplies for the army to outposts up north. We will be leaving for Montana Territory any day now. If you check with the major at your headquarters, he can show you the arrangements," Fern said.

"You two-bit cowboys. Get out of my way." He pulled the reins and galloped down the street.

"Never mind him," Fern said to Noah. "Look at you!" They embraced again. "You made it back alive. I guess I can thank the Almighty for that. Come on, you look like you could eat. Then you can tell me all about it."

Fern led Noah to an eating house and ordered most of the limited menu. Noah was ravenous, eating two full plates before entertaining any questions from Fern. Noah washed down a second plate of biscuits, meat, and gravy with a glass of fresh milk and then slouched in his chair. He rubbed his belly and thought of napping. Minutes became hours as he addressed every question from Fern. The two friends laughed and talked, expressing their elation over being together again.

Fern stared at Noah with a condescending scowl. "So, the Comanche and the wolf just rode away, huh? And did I hear you right? The Comanche actually shot Hamilton in the leg and saved you? Now, why on earth would he do that and then attack Adobe Walls?"

"I never said he attacked Adobe Walls," Noah replied. "I said he rode away. But he turned those other Comanches away and kept them from coming after me. Don't ask me why. I don't know."

"I see. It sounds like you impressed him. You've always had a strange gift when it comes to wildlife. But wolves?"

"I know," Noah replied. "It just felt right. I can't explain it."

"But?"

"There was something there with the Comanche, Fern. Like what you and I have. A bond. It's as though I knew him. And the wolf . . . I don't know. I guess it was friendly. It could have killed me if it wanted to."

Fern slapped Noah on his shoulder. "But it didn't. Sounds like your guardian angel was working overtime for your sorry hide. That is interesting that you ran into that preacher. He probably saved you from becoming a Great Plains coyote dinner. I wish I could have met him and thanked him for getting you back. And a cattle drive? What a coincidence." Fern snickered.

"I know that look," Noah stated. "What have you gotten us into now? And what is this about cattle and supplies to Montana Territory? I barely survived going south to Adobe Walls, and now you want to head north for another one?"

"Calm down. This could be the one opportunity we have been waiting for. A steady contract with the army and a perfect fit for you."

"A cowboy?" Noah asked.

"The working title is a security detail for supplies and cattle," Fern said. "They also want to establish a cow town in Montana and build it up. Our job is to help make sure all the goods and livestock get there in one piece."

"In other words, we are hired guns."

"Security!" Fern yelled. He looked at the waitress. "And, on occasion, cowboys."

Noah scoffed at Fern. "Maybe I should go find that captain and take him up on his offer. You keep this up, and we will be doing everything from blacksmithing to shoveling manure."

Fern paid the waitress and led Noah outside. He wrapped one arm around Noah and whispered while they walked. "Listen, when we get this outfit to Montana, we will never need another job again."

"So, genius. Convince me. What's your plan?"

"After we finish this job, we are going to have our own ranch—lock, stock, and barrel!" Fern exclaimed.

"Since when are you a rancher?"

"I'm not. And neither are you. We will build it up, work it for a few years, and then sell it off for a handsome price. The beginnings of a fortune."

"You've always had an eye for business. But in Montana Territory?" Noah asked. "There is nothing up there, and those winters are brutal."

"Quit whining," Fern injected. "So it's cold. We've had worse on the plains, hunting winter hides for months on end. I'm an opportunist, and this is a great opportunity for both of us. And with the buffalo dwindling, this may be the *only* opportunity for us. Besides, you always want to stay away from people, right? Well, this place is off the map. Come on. There's someone I want you to meet."

They approached the stable yard and entered the barn. Several covered wagons filled with supplies were staged in the adjacent lot. Men scurried between the rigs, making final preparations for departure.

Fern escorted Noah to a group of men and stopped next to a redheaded Irishman. Noah towered over the man. His red beard appeared as fire in the sunlight. The man acknowledged Fern and faced Noah with a stout posture.

"Noah, this is Patrick Walsh, the trail boss," Fern said.

Patrick sized up Noah and said, "You look young, boy. How do I know you won't falter on this drive?"

Noah asked Fern, "What's a falter?"

Fern injected. "He is strong, Mr. Walsh. He will work hard for you."

"He is working for the army. We all are. Make sure you both understand that. And you had better understand that I have no room for boys who do not work hard and earn their share. Do you hear me, boy?" Patrick asked.

Noah gritted his teeth. "Fern, why do good men call me 'son' and weak fools call me 'boy'?" he asked as he brushed his hand over the heel of his revolver.

Fern stepped between Noah and Patrick and said, "Stop it! What has gotten into you, Noah?"

"More of the same!" Noah yelled. "I get a glimpse of heaven riding here with Jerill Oren—a respectable man, a true leader. And now it's back to the usual—another narrow-minded pretender with a big mouth." Noah stared at Patrick as he yearned to pull his revolver. "So, you have no room for boys. Well, I have no room for fools who shoot their mouth off, not knowing who they are dealing with!"

Fern forced Noah away and coaxed him to gather his gear.

"Please excuse him, Mr. Walsh. He's tired. Like I said, we were buffalo hunters by trade, and Noah just finished a cattle drive to Dodge City. He was also at Adobe Walls when it was attacked. He's been through a lot lately."

"He is a feisty one, isn't he? And he had better watch that temper of his," Patrick said. "Otherwise, he is perfect for the job. No fear, which is exactly what we need. Well done, Mr. Raul. However, I advise he not call me a fool ever again." He noticed their guns. "How handy are you with those?"

"We've made our living with them so far," Fern said.

"Shooting buffalo only?" Patrick asked.

Noah grabbed his gear and yelled loud enough for Patrick to hear him. "Or anything dumb enough to shoot back!"

Patrick chuckled at Noah and addressed Fern. "Isn't he a bit young to be talking like that?"

Fern watched Noah walk away. "Not when he doesn't have a choice."

CHAPTER 4

June 1876

Noah leaned against the only tree on the grassy hilltop. Its branches provided enough shade for a pleasant noonday view. His horse grazed on the other side of the tree as he saw a grove of trees nestled along the winding banks of a distant river. The leaves shimmered in the sunlight through the churning wind. After two years, the rolling terrain and cool summer breeze of Montana Territory were still foreign to him. He was used to the fiery heat and dry, dusty range of the southern plains. The lush, green hills and endless blue sky seemed inconceivable compared to the land he was used to. But with each passing day, he surrendered more fondly to the frontier paradise around him.

Hundreds of cattle grazed in the valley. The herd had tripled in size since the long drive from Dodge City two years earlier. The meager farm became a respectable ranch and a major supplier of beef to most of Montana Territory. Noah began to appreciate his role with the ranch. Gone were the days of depleting buffalo herds and searching for work. He took solace in the ranch's mission to nurture and protect livestock. Noah enjoyed the peace and solitude of his work and the area. The winters tested his resolve against high snowdrifts and frigid temperatures. The vastness and beauty of the territory provided great appeal, but his heart remained with the southern plains.

The approach of a horse ended his solitude. He dreaded the interference, not ready to reengage with the duties of the day. The rider slowed and trotted in front of Noah, who shielded his eyes to see Fern staring down at him. Noah watched his friend for a lengthy moment, hoping that the irritation his presence caused would be obvious.

"You're blocking my view," Noah said.

"It's hard to see with your eyes closed. Quit napping and come with me," Fern replied.

"I'm going to count to three. And then I'm going to shoot you," Noah stated.

Fern ignored him. "I mean it. Mount up. I have something to show you."

Noah retrieved his horse and followed Fern. They traversed the hills to a distant rise overlooking another valley. Fern had Noah dismount. They reached the summit and knelt in the grass. A small herd of buffalo grazed nearby. The sight invigorated Noah with nostalgia. The picturesque scene consumed him with memories. He remembered when he would have watched the herd with a hunter's passion. But now he witnessed the noble creatures as a tranquil treasure of the past.

"When did you find them?" Noah asked.

"A few days ago, when I was rounding up some cattle near here," Fern replied. "I figured you might want to see them. What a great reminder of the good ol' days, huh?"

"Looks like a few hundred of them."

"It's the largest herd I've seen in this area. I recall seeing a smaller herd when we arrived here two years ago," Fern added. "But nothing like this since then."

"It seems the same everywhere, from what I hear," Noah replied. "Since the Comanches down south surrendered last year, even the tribes are fewer."

"I don't know about that," Fern said. "There is a lot of commotion in town. The army is massing in force south of here. The local tribes are all stirred up. There could be trouble."

Noah continued admiring the buffalo. "They won't be happy until everything is gone."

"Regardless, the army must eat. They ordered some beef. Mr. Walsh wants us to lead a small herd to Fort Ellis. We leave today. Two cowhands are going with us. I told him we could handle it, but he wants added security."

"I'll be along shortly," Noah said. He admired the buffalo with an altered perspective. The wandering animals portrayed a natural connection with the land. Noah began to appreciate the giant beasts for how they belonged across the plains. For the first time, he felt concern for them. The decreasing numbers were becoming more evident. For a moment, he realized with subtle dismay that he could be watching the permanent demise of the buffalo in his lifetime. And his remorse was due to his contribution to it.

"They are a beautiful sight," Fern said.

"Yes, they are," Noah replied. In contemplation, he remained drawn to the herd. "Do you regret hunting them like we did?"

Fern mounted his horse. "No, that was our livelihood. We did what we had to do at that time."

"They are nearly gone."

"Not all of them. Cattle have taken over. There may still be a few buffalo hunters out there, but only the larger outfits."

"I would hate to see them disappear. They are a part of the plains," Noah said.

"What's with you? You're beginning to sound like one of those conservationists back East."

Noah crossed his arms. "I don't see the reasoning in hunting an animal until it is completely gone. That makes no sense."

"There is nothing we can do about that today. Come on. Mr. Walsh is waiting." Fern turned his horse and headed back toward the ranch, but Noah continued to watch the buffalo. They migrated along a grass-covered slope, enjoying the feast of greenery. He watched a young calf playing outside the herd. It bounded through the grass, separating from the others.

Then Noah saw movement at the top of the slope. Two ears perked in the tall grass. He watched as the head of a gray wolf rose above the foliage. It spied the calf from its elevated view. Noah noticed the herd meandering along unaware. The calf ran farther away from protection. The wolf angled its head and stood. Noah gasped as five more wolves stood with it.

"Uh-oh," Noah muttered. He looked at his horse. A gray wolf lay prone in the grass a few yards from him. Noah froze. Fear raced through him as the wolf snarled. Noah moved slowly next to his mount. His horse was facing away from the wolf, not realizing the imposing threat. Noah calmed his horse and located his rifle, which was strapped in the carrier. The wolf remained still, watching every move.

Noah peered at the wolf. He made eye contact with the predator and focused on it. Its ears had noticeable yellow tips that contrasted against its dark fur.

Curious about the situation, Noah reached for his saddlebag and opened a large portion of wrapped jerky. He looked at the wolf and took a bite of the dried meat. The wolf twitched its nose with sudden interest. Noah stepped forward and spread several long strips of the jerky on the ground. The wolf inched closer, keeping its stare on Noah. He unhitched his horse and slapped the saddle. The mount galloped down the slope, still unaware of the wolf.

The wolf approached the jerky. After a few sniffs, the sleek predator checked both directions and then snatched the meat in its fangs. It devoured the jerky in seconds. Noah peeked from the tree. The wolf licked its snout, eager for more. It angled its head, portraying a sense of concentration.

Noah stepped from the tree and knelt. He remembered his encounter with the wolf at Adobe Walls. Relying on hope, he extended his hand with another piece of jerky.

The wolf agonized over the offer. Noah watched as it battled with its better judgment. Surrendering to temptation, it finally stepped closer to Noah.

Noah gently coaxed the wolf. It came within feet of his hand and lunged at the meat. The swift predator ripped the jerky away and bounded over the rise.

Noah followed. He crested the slope to see numerous buffalo surrounding the calf. The wolf pack was attacking the herd with daring strikes. Several buffalo cows circled the calf, desperately ushering it ahead. Noah saw a huge bull charge an unknowing wolf. It slammed its horns head-on into the wolf's side. The animal howled as the bull raised it high into the air and flung it several feet away.

The injured predator limped away with high-pitched whimpers. The engagement continued for several minutes. The bull struck again, severely hurting another wolf before a second bull arrived to challenge the remaining pack. Depleted from injuries, the pack retreated. The two bulls hustled after the fleeing herd.

Noah watched the wolf pack's surprising withdrawal. He retrieved his horse and noticed the pack rallying around a dark object. A buffalo cow had become a sacrifice for the young calf. The wolves pounced on the carcass with relentless satisfaction. The feeding frenzy was heard throughout the valley.

Noah knew the primitive scene would be like many he had witnessed before. The gallant effort by both species proved to be another episode of the natural order. He had just knelt to watch the pack feed when he felt a sudden nudge at his back. He saw the wolf staring at him. Stunned, he positioned himself and prepared for the worst. The wolf expressed interest, waiting for Noah to make the next move. Gambling with fate, he extended his hand again. The animal sniffed for inspection. Noah scratched the wolf behind its ears.

He saw the wildness in its eyes and its untamed stature of dominance and strength. The moment was exhilarating. He rubbed its head. The wolf remained unmoving, relishing the unique treatment. It bumped Noah's hand with its nose. The serenity of the moment astonished Noah. Not since the wolf at Adobe Walls had he felt such a presence. It was an experience he could not explain then, but now it was happening again. Confusion led to intrigue as the mysterious connection became less of a coincidence and more of a bond.

Fifty cattle moved in unison through a valley heading west. Fern and Noah led the drive, with two cowhands providing security and rounding up strays. The low number of cattle allowed for better timeliness for the short trip. To minimize delays, the men carried their own food stores, avoiding a cumbersome chuck wagon. The ample supply of water and grass along the route sustained the cattle to their destination.

"Why so small a herd?" Noah asked. "Is this worth it?"

"The army is coming through the area," Fern replied. "They wanted twenty head at first, but Mr. Walsh told them no less than fifty for a sale. When he owns the only large ranch in the area, I guess he can do that. He is making money out here, for sure. Not to mention getting the sole contract with the army for beef. I have no doubt horses will be next."

"How far are we going?" Noah asked.

"Fort Ellis. This will be a short drive," Fern stated. "We will head south and use the Yellowstone and Bighorn Rivers along the way. Less work for us."

"Whatever you say. You're the trail boss," Noah replied. "I noticed the ranch seemed deserted when we left. Where did everyone go?"

"Mr. Walsh said some of the men quit. All this talk about Indians and the army scared them off. They don't want the responsibility of losing a herd. I think that is also why Mr. Walsh kept this drive to fifty. It may be more work for us with fewer cowhands, but it is more money for us too." Fern looked ahead. "Let's scout the terrain and see where it leads."

Fern signaled to the cowhands and rode on with Noah. They located a river and mapped their course. The route to Fort Ellis appeared easy compared to previous drives. Satisfied with the direction, they identified landmarks and left for the herd.

"Fern! Listen . . ." Noah stopped his horse. "Do you hear that?"

Fern slowed his mount. "Those sound like gunshots."

"Hundreds of them!" Noah exclaimed. "Can you tell where they're coming from?"

"Follow me!" Fern yelled.

They spurred their mounts along an adjacent rise. Both men stared as a thousand Indians massed below a distant hill.

"That has got to be every tribe in the territory," Fern said.

"I've never seen a hunting party that size. I didn't know there were that many tribes in Montana Territory. Do you see any buffalo?" Both men watched as the gunfire intensified. "Are they firing at that group on the hill?" Noah asked.

"Those are soldiers."

"It doesn't look like many of them," Noah replied. They struggled to make sense of the scene. "What are they doing? Are they . . ."

Fern stood in his stirrups as panic overcame him. "That's no hunt."

"What?" Noah asked, noticing Fern's anxious posture.

Fern heeled his horse and yanked the reins to the right. "That's a battle!" Fern motivated his mount after the herd. He waved at the cowhands, trying not to alarm the cattle. "Turn the herd! Stampede to the north!"

"Fern!" Noah shouted and pointed westward. A line of mounted Indians watched them from a hill.

"We've got to move the herd!"

"They're going to attack! We don't have time, Fern!"

Fern saw the two cowhands abandon the herd and flee. "Start a stampede," he said. "It's our only chance to save them." Fern held his revolver and fired several rounds. The startled cattle dispersed in multiple directions. Chaos enveloped the valley as cows scattered across the terrain.

Noah yelled at Fern, "They're coming!"

The line of attackers converged on their location. The cattle slowed and formed meandering groups throughout the valley. Out of options, both men fled northward, firing their revolvers. The second volley jolted the cattle into panicked clusters. The men hollered as the stampede took shape. The cows assembled and charged aimlessly at the oncoming Indians. The bovine assault forced the Indians to bypass the rushing horde. Fern and Noah took advantage of the clamoring barrier and sprinted northeast, away from the attack.

"What do you mean they never showed up? They left before we did," Fern exclaimed. "Noah and I watched them ride away before we had a chance to tell them anything."

Patrick Walsh stood next to the window of his ranch house. He peered outside with failing patience. Fern and Noah finished dinner and remained at the table. Patrick thought of various questions for the men. As a seasoned rancher, he'd learned from generations before him that patience prevailed when all else could not be controlled. His experience with weather, disease, and drought had steadied him for life as a rancher. Nature alone had taught him several lessons in patience. But after his many decades of endurance, he was simply tired of the constant tribulation.

"As I said, the two cowhands never came back to the ranch. I entrusted you with their safety. I don't know if they are alive or dead." Fern became disgusted as Patrick continued. "Now, about my cattle. All fifty of them? The whole herd is gone? You couldn't save even a few?"

"We were fortunate to save ourselves," Fern replied.

"What made you drive them that far south anyway?" Patrick asked.

"Water. We talked about that before we left."

"Don't sass me!" Patrick warned. "Did you think to scout the way ahead before leading the herd in that direction? Anyone who has ever been on a cattle drive knows to do that, even a first-time trail boss I thought was experienced."

"Of course we did! But by the time we saw the Indians riding toward us, it was too late." Realizing the debate was becoming more of a fight, Fern changed the subject. "What happened out there anyway?"

Patrick returned to the window. "From what I hear, it was a massacre. Most of the Seventh Cavalry was killed by several tribes in the area. I don't know everything that happened yet. But it seems you two witnessed a major battle. The army has been searching all over, making a mess of things. I haven't seen troop movements like this since before Appomattox, back in '65. I'm sure this is only the beginning."

"I can't believe we nearly drove a herd into a battle," Fern said.

Patrick swung around from the window. "You might as well have! My cows are gone. The army will adjust for their losses. Who will adjust for mine? No one!"

Fern stood from the table. "We will go look for the herd. I have no idea where they will be or if any of them survived, but we can try."

"Do what you can. I have the help I have left watching the herds on the ranch day and night. I can't spare any more hands."

"Noah and I will leave first thing in the morning," Fern said.

Patrick leaned toward Fern. His lip quivered from anger. "You two can saddle your horses and go find my cows right now. I lost a lot of money in that fifty head. I am not going to lose that contract with Fort Ellis. Let me be clear: You two can find my cows, or you can pay me for the losses."

Noah stood from the table and kicked his chair against the wall. "What? We rode into a battle! It was not our fault."

Fern ignored Noah's outburst and addressed Patrick instead. "We will do what we can."

Patrick grabbed his cowboy hat. "I'm going to check on the other hands and make sure they aren't costing me more money too. If there is one thing I will not tolerate, it is the hired help abandoning my herds!"

Fern escorted Noah outside. They packed their saddlebags with every belonging and rode away in search of the cattle.

Noah slowed his horse at the distant sound of gunfire. He steered north and rode to investigate, with Fern close behind. They traversed a ridge bordering the only valley on the ranch. Both men stopped at an overlook. Noah stood in his stirrups in astonishment at the sight before him.

Numerous dead buffalo littered the valley floor. A few survivors searched through the carcasses, seeming confused about what direction to go. Several gunshots exploded from the other side of the ridge. The remaining buffalo staggered and fell. Their lifeless bodies rested next to other dead buffalo, creating a morbid scene.

Noah watched three men reload their rifles. A calf called from the center of the carnage. One man sighted the animal and fired.

"No!" Noah yelled. He and Fern approached the three men. "What are you doing? Are you out of your minds?"

Patrick dashed in on his mount from behind Noah and Fern, then yanked his reins to a sudden stop. "What are you two doing here? I told you to go find my cattle!"

"Why are you killing these buffalo?" Noah asked.

Patrick spotted another buffalo trying to escape the valley. "Get out of the way!" he hollered at Noah, then aimed his rifle and fired at the escaping buffalo. The animal slammed to the ground, unmoving. Patrick rested his rifle on his hip and spoke with bitter regard. "The army wants them all dead. I guess you can consider this fallout from that battle you saw. It's no matter. The worthless things were eating my grazing pastures anyway."

Noah saw the massacre. Never had he witnessed the brutality and waste from so close. The dead buffalo appeared as black scars cut across the valley. He surveyed the area with remorse. He remembered a hunt during which he and Fern had found a mass slaughter. The buffalo carcasses were stripped of their hides and tongues. The mounds of meat were left to rot in the sun. He continued to observe the valley and noticed a smaller object lying in the grass.

Patrick saw Noah looking at it. "I shot that thing yesterday. It kept nosing around the ranch. One less varmint to deal with."

His heart sank as he spurred his horse. Noah stopped over the lifeless body of a gray wolf. His eyes were drawn to the distinctive yellow tips of the animal's ears. Rage engulfed him. He heeled his mount in the direction of the men on the ridge. They watched Noah's rapid approach. Before they could react, Noah rammed his horse into Patrick and his mount. The impact rolled Patrick onto the ground. His mount whinnied and bucked from the attack. Noah jumped from his saddle and ran toward Patrick.

"You didn't have to kill it!" Noah shouted. "Any of them! We could have driven them onto the plains. That wolf wasn't bothering your cattle. It was after the buffalo—the buffalo you killed!"

Patrick moaned from the hard fall. He glared at Noah and drew his revolver. The sight of the weapon created an instinctive response in Noah. His posture altered from uncontrolled anger to overwhelming intimidation. With mesmerizing speed, Noah presented his weapon and fired before Patrick extended his arm. The round struck Patrick's revolver at an angle, ricocheting off the metal barrel. The revolver launched backward, hitting Patrick in the head. He fell to the ground. Patrick bellowed in pain as Noah walked closer. He aimed his weapon at Patrick's head.

"I didn't miss." Noah cocked the hammer. "And the next shot won't either."

"That's enough!" Fern yelled. "Lower your revolver, Noah."

Noah saw the other cowhands react and shifted his aim at them instead. "Either of you try anything, and you will join those buffalo down there."

Fern moved his mount between Noah and the men. "Get on your horse."

Patrick stood, holding his hand. "You two get out of here! Don't come on my property again. Do you hear me?"

Noah fired two shots at Patrick's feet. "Don't follow us." He holstered his revolver and climbed onto the saddle.

Fern led Noah safely away from the ranch. He refrained from talking. They rode for several miles before reaching a river. Fern steered them to a small tree grove nestled along the bank. He dismounted and tied the reins. Fern walked to the edge of the water with his hands on his hips. Dreading what was to come, Noah followed suit and stood next to him. Moments passed before Fern mustered any words.

"I swear, Noah. You are pushing me to the limit. I know you have been through a lot, both now and in your past. But what you did back there..."

"It was a matter of time, Fern, and you know it," Noah said. "He was asking for it."

Fern shoved Noah, knocking him to the ground. He stood over Noah with failing restraint. "You provoked that! That could have gotten out of control!"

"Only for them!"

Fern threw his cowboy hat. "That doesn't matter! What matters is that you *wanted* it to get out of control. You wanted to fight them." Fern ran his hand over his forehead. "You can't keep drawing your gun on people every time you get angry. And you get angry all the time! I'm sick of it, Noah."

Noah stood and brushed off his pants. "They didn't have to kill them, Fern. They killed them for no reason."

"What's that to you? The army wants the buffalo dead. Killing all the buffalo starves the tribes. You saw what happened at the Little Bighorn. This is not only a slaughter. It's politics. There is nothing you can do." Noah looked at the river as Fern continued. "And what was that wolf all about? You were in a fit of rage. I am beginning to wonder about you." Noah gritted his teeth at the thought of the dead wolf. "You are scaring me. I saw your eyes, and I know you. You never go on the defensive, and your lack of fear isn't normal." Fern paused, "You wanted to kill Mr. Walsh. You did everything possible to provoke it except pull the trigger for him." Fern stepped away to compose himself. "Curse you, Noah. That's murder!"

Noah watched the river's current coast along. Small rapids and curling ripples calmed him. The rolling water soothed his thoughts and carried away his anguish. He searched his mind for a genuine response.

"Remember my trip to Adobe Walls, when the Comanche attacked?" Fern did not reply. "Those men I rode with shot at everything. Any animal, for no reason. I wanted to kill every one of those men." Noah surrendered to his memories. "There was a wolf watching us pass by. It wasn't bothering anything. They shot at it, and I stopped them. Then the Comanche attacked. I realized later that the Comanche were headed for that camp near Adobe Walls. We just happened to be in their way. They hadn't expected us. I stopped those men from killing that wolf. One of the Comanches must have seen me do it. I thought I was trapped, and a Comanche let me go. But before he did, he led the wolf to me." Noah's eyes began to tear. "I don't know why that Comanche did that. He said something to me in his language. I didn't understand him, but he said it in a meaningful way, like you would. That was when I realized we were wrong, Fern. I was wrong for killing those animals on the plains. I am as much to blame as those men back there with Walsh."

"Why does this bother you so much?" Fern asked.

"I have no purpose in this life. I just exist. I ride the plains and shoot buffalo. I kill. For what? Some livelihood?" Noah cleared his throat. "I'd rather shoot men! At least then I would be saving the buffalo instead of killing them." Noah paused. Fern watched his expression transform as if he were possessed. Noah faced in the direction of the ranch. "Why did he kill that wolf!" He yanked his revolver and fired multiple times in the direction of the ranch. Fern watched his friend with concern as Noah dropped the revolver.

Fern stepped closer, allowing the moment to pass. His sorrow for Noah provided previously forgotten clarity about the source of his friend's emotional agony. Remorse consumed him as he realized that Noah's infuriated demeanor was another testimony of his haunting past. Remembering the day they met and the chosen role he had performed without hesitation, Fern fulfilled the calling once again and rescued Noah from himself.

"Look at me." Fern spoke with a firm tone. He had learned from previous experiences how to connect with Noah as a wise and caring friend. "You cannot keep holding on to the past. You must learn to let go of your regret. It is destroying you."

Noah rubbed his eyes. "I don't know how." Tears streamed as he raised his head toward the sky. "I'll never kill another wild animal again."

Fern retrieved the revolver and holstered it for him. He placed his hand on Noah's shoulder and squeezed gently.

"I know."

CHAPTER 5

August 1886

The wind drifted over the viewable landscape of Montana Territory, appearing as waves in the dense grasses. The summer warmth and recent rains nourished a late-season greenery. The hills and contours extended beyond the horizon. The vastness of the land complemented the endless sky. The span of the territory, with its many shades of blues, tans, and greens, portrayed an earthly scene unrivaled across the Great Plains.

Noah watched the setting from his frequented location on a hilltop. The overlook was his place of solitude, where he could witness the grand expanse. Often, he pictured the view with the perception of an artist. He envied the gift of painters. He dreamed of having the talent to capture the beauty before him on canvas and cherish it for days to come. The limitations of sight and memory beckoned his weekly visits to the hill. The repetition ensured a vivid recollection of the peaceful scene within his yearning mind.

Noah watched the only known buffalo herd remaining in the area. Its feeble numbers appeared to have dwindled each time he saw them. The location was remote, and it was too costly for hunters to pursue the herd for such a small payout. Poachers were rumored to be an increasing threat, but isolation and a strict trust in conservation protected the roaming herd. Noah's previous livelihood had depended upon the relentless hunting of the great beasts without remorse. He pushed those memories far into the recesses of his mind, eager to forget the past. His renewed vigor came from an appreciation for their place in nature and a determination to protect what remaining few he could.

The buffalo herd was free to graze about the area and stay hidden. The nearest civilized town was several miles away. Developing ranches had gradually expanded across the territory, further encroaching upon the open prairie. Noah knew his only means of protecting the buffalo was distance. The ongoing attempt to hide the wandering herd proved desperate and uncontrollable. He knew it would be a matter of time before they were discovered by any number of unfortunate circumstances. His problem was that he could do nothing about it.

Noah mounted his horse and meandered home. In the ten years since leaving Patrick Walsh, he and Fern had established a thriving ranch on a few select tracts of land still available for settlement. Their operation was small compared to the larger, more established outfits throughout the territory. To compete for prices and demand, they raised horses and cattle, selling mostly to the army and other ranches that were trying to expand. They worked for every meal and were consumed with chores and tasks that seemed to multiply without end. The dream of going from ranching to riches became a futile and frigid reality with the first Montana winter. Half of their assets died. The remaining animals required all their funds to survive disease. Nothing came easy. And for Noah, it easily led to nothing.

As Noah rode farther, the ranch finally came within view. He looked at the modest dwelling and corral with spite. Their decade in the making had become an entrapment—not of his friendship with Fern or their investment in the ranch, but of his life. He despised the change from surviving life when he was younger to sustaining life at the present. Age and time had become his enemies.

He remembered his early years and the parental teachings that, over time, he'd managed to ignore. Faith and prayer, for him, were never viable options when combating the lessons of life that brought harsh change on every occasion. Reality was his mainstay, for it was all he knew. Riding to the place they'd built with hope had become hopeless. He felt hostage to a situation that he had no means of escaping. Previous ambition and confidence had been destroyed by the very reality that he relied upon. It had become a life he did not know how to change. As life passed by, age and time surrendered to fear.

A strong gust ripped the cowboy hat off his head. It was tossed in the wind and bounced across the ground. Noah slid off the saddle and ran after it. The hat rolled along as the draft took it from Noah. Then the hat launched into the air and dropped over a rise in the terrain. Too far from his horse, Noah trudged up the hill in pursuit. He reached the summit and, out of breath, rested his hands on his knees.

"Is this yours?"

Noah saw a man on the other side of the hill holding his cowboy hat. Fern sat on his mount next to the man, holding the reins to the man's horse. Still heaving for air, Noah prepared to respond before Fern engaged in the conversation with an eager grin.

"Good thing you belted your pants!" Fern said with a chuckle. "Let's hope a storm doesn't blow in."

"Shut up, Fern." Noah took his hat from the man. "Much obliged." He extended his hand and said, "Noah Wrath."

"John Bruce. Happy to help."

Fern continued his joyous harassment. "Might want to tuck your shirt in. The wind's pickin' up."

"Mr. Bruce," Noah interjected. "I see you have little regard for the company you keep."

"I've been putting up with you for longer than I care to count. Mr. Bruce, I'm going to fetch my friend's horse over there before the wind gets ahold of it too. Please make acquaintances until I get back."

John chuckled at the men. "You two certainly do not need enemies."

Fern retrieved Noah's mount, and the men rode to the ranch house. Fern presented fresh elk venison he'd purchased in town and complemented it with biscuits and gravy. The men feasted with hot coffee and light conversation. Fern surprised them with a huckleberry pie a neighbor had made for dessert. The men treated themselves to hefty portions and emptied the coffee pot. Satisfied with the substantial meal, they relaxed in their seats as the discussion became more formal.

"I didn't know the country had a national museum," Noah stated. "You are a long way from home, John."

"It was quite a journey from Washington," John replied. "There is a lot of somewhere between here and there. I work indirectly for the United States National Museum. I'm looking for direction in finding wild buffalo for some representatives of the museum. They plan to visit Montana Territory later this year. They need specimens for the museum, and, frankly, they need all the help they can get."

"Specimens?" Noah asked.

"Yes. And they are willing to pay handsomely for any information, a guide, anything for good-quality animals to take back East," John responded.

Noah straightened in his seat as Fern anticipated his reaction. "Alive?" Noah asked.

"That is for my clients to decide."

Noah pushed away from the table and prepared to leave. "Then we cannot help you." He reached for the door.

"Noah, wait," Fern said.

Noah replied, "You know where I stand with this."

"They are trying to preserve some buffalo."

"By mounting their heads on some city wall back East! Am I right, John?" Noah yelled. "Fern and I hunted buffalo for years. We killed hundreds of them and watched countless other hunters do the same. Some killed them for sport and left them lying out there to rot. We aided in their demise. I have to live with that. And now, you arrive and want me to help you finish them off? Forget it!" Noah opened the door.

"Noah . . . Mr. Wrath. Please wait," John said. Fern gestured for Noah to calm down and return to his seat. "I can see you are passionate about the preservation of wildlife. It is admirable. Fernando told me the history you both share. What he said reminded me of a phrase I have found to be quite true in my life. 'Sometimes in life, we tend to change our perspective the longer we live life.' Maybe that has occurred with you. I don't know. But he also said that you fair rather well with various weaponry for defensive purposes."

"Defensive purposes?" Noah asked.

"Shut up and let him finish," Fern demanded.

John saw the escalating tension between Noah and Fern. "I noticed you both have a legitimate operation here and an appreciation for horses, mules, some cattle . . . You two appear to be fully capable of handling yourselves. And your past employment endeavors obviously solidify those skills. Good for you. Good for both of you."

Noah became impatient. "Mr. Bruce, is there more to this?"

"Oh yes," John replied. He'd made the misleading impression that he was a common bystander. But now he'd revealed that he was a person of position. Intrigue consumed Noah as John spoke with emphasis. "I ask that you both keep what I am about to say between us, as it is rather premature to mention. But sometimes, timing can be, well, unexpected." John continued with a noticeable authority to his demeanor. "There is a society of people—whose names I cannot reveal for discretionary concerns—who continue to organize across the country. This society is very influential. The members are very powerful, with positions in politics and business. They have unlimited financial resources. You name it, they can do it. Their goal is to create sanctuaries in various locations throughout the West. Very soon, legislation will be passed to legalize the provision of wildlife in the Yellowstone National Park."

"Wildlife?" Fern asked.

John noticed the sudden interest. "Buffalo, elk, deer—any native animal needing sanctuary in a natural habitat."

"I didn't hear you mention any predator wildlife on this sanctuary of yours," Noah said. John did not reply. Noah detected the strange avoidance of his statement and pondered if it was intentional. Guarding his thoughts, he continued with a question. "How exactly does this interest us?"

John tapped his fingers on the table and deliberately delayed his response to make a meaningful impression. "There is another provision that I believe you and Fernando can greatly assist us with regarding the wildlife sanctuary. Poachers continue to be a nuisance in Yellowstone National Park. With this new legislation, we will, for the first time, be able to enforce the protection of wildlife, ensuring a thriving and secure habitat. What I am looking for, Noah, are experienced and trustworthy associates capable of executing this noble and well-compensated provision." John paused again to allow his words to resonate. "Do I have your interest now, gentlemen?"

Fern cleared his throat and leaned back in his seat. Moments passed before he looked at Noah. Noah covered his mouth with his hand, hiding a subtle grin.

"It sounds like you want hired guns," Fern said.

"Not hired guns, Fernando. Hired protectors to work for an elite membership," John replied. "It is a process, but we are expanding our influence yearly. In this case, however, we need a daily influence."

"You mentioned enforcement. Are you looking for some kind of lawman?" Noah asked.

"No," John replied. "Matters at Yellowstone are challenging. Enforcement will be up to the army. A unit will be located within the park boundaries to provide a deterrent. Your role would be to ensure the protected wildlife thrives without incident. You, along with other members of various influences, will determine certain areas within the park where you will nurture and protect the wildlife placed there so they may recover and multiply. A protective overseer, you might say."

"How protective?" Noah asked.

"For you, whatever the moment may require." John reclined in his seat. "But I ask that any excessive force be used at the army's discretion. We do not need any unnecessary, shall we say, complications to our work."

"That shouldn't be a problem. I speak for both of us," Fern said.

"Good. I consider this settled then," John replied.

"When do you need us there?" Fern asked.

"At the present time, only one of you is required at Yellowstone to work as our liaison," John answered. Noah and Fern were surprised. "Noah, I would prefer that to be you. You fit our needs there, and I am confident that you will make an immediate influence. There will be a small contingent of our members there to meet you and get you acquainted with the operation. And having gotten to know you, however briefly, I believe you will find a welcome contentment once you see what we are working to accomplish there. I can have you on the payroll immediately if you can depart by the end of next week."

John directed his attention to Fern. "I would appreciate you joining me for a brief visit in Washington. Your obvious aptitude for business will be most beneficial to some members of the society. Once we have everything in place, we will reevaluate our positions and proceed from there."

John paused. "Understand, gentlemen, that we do not offer these opportunities to just anyone. Trust is our mainstay. Only the most dedicated and genuine of heart are selected for our endeavor. Once you are accepted, you will become associated with a very prestigious society. And I assure you, our compensation for your unique services and dedication will not leave you in need. You will be very well paid." John concluded the conversation. "Any questions, gentlemen?"

Noah had a perplexed expression. He waved, indicating acceptance, and nodded at John. He sat without a response. Fern was astonished at his reaction. He knew the conversation had brought up questions that Noah did not want to ask in front of John. What he did not expect was the concession on Noah's face. Fern felt regret. Over the years of knowing his friend and interpreting his mannerisms in every situation, he had never seen Noah like this before. He prepared for the expected engagement with him. Waiting seconds for a possible response, Fern filled the void and extended his hand to John. The men exchanged pleasantries as John departed for his mount.

Fern took a deep breath and returned to his seat across from Noah, who appeared defeated. Noah rubbed his hand over the smooth wooden tabletop. Fern waited for him to say something. An awkward minute passed before Fern surrendered to the situation and engaged with Noah.

"I know that was a lot to hear."

Noah remained disinterested, shifting his hand back and forth over the table. "If that went any faster, I'd say we were hit by a steam engine."

Fern searched for the right words, hoping to control the fragile conversation. "He had to hurry. He needed to meet his guide to find the buffalo. I'm glad he made time for us."

"I thought he was trying to *hire* a guide," Noah said. Fern saw the realization in Noah's eyes and knew the moment that he'd dreaded was upon him. "You knew about this!"

Fern raised his hands in defense. "All right, don't get crazy on me. Yes, I met him earlier in town on a supply run. We got to talking, and he told me what he was looking for. After hearing what he had to say, I wanted him to meet you."

"You were sold on this from the beginning, weren't you?" Noah asked.

"Come on, Noah. This is a good opportunity for both of us."

"For you! Washington? Did you agree to that too?"

"He asked me earlier. I'm interested. And for the amount of money he is offering, I'm very interested," Fern said.

"You sold us out. You, me, the ranch, all of it. Why?"

"Don't give me that, Noah! Let's face facts here if you are going to go down that path. You aren't happy here, and you know it. Neither one of us is a rancher, especially you. We might as well be settlers, the way we mope around here like two old men fighting over the rocking chair at the end of the day. You spend more time out there on that hill of yours, watching the horizon and dreaming of what could be or what could have been. You were your happiest riding around on the plains, wild and free, without a care in the world. The day that ended, you became miserable, and you haven't changed since then."

"I don't need you to speak for me. That wasn't fair," Noah replied.

"You were not going to speak for yourself. You have given up, Noah. You are nothing like you used to be back in our buffalo-hunting days. I mean, look at you! You are mad all the time, you complain about everything, and you're never happy. All you want to do is argue or fight everyone who comes around. You have turned yourself into one big pain in the butt, and I'm tired of it!"

Noah stared at the table and stopped moving his hand. "At least now I know the real reason you are going to Washington." He stood and approached the door.

Fern grabbed his arm. "I don't like what you have become. You hate life and everything about it. And what scares me the most is that you hate your own life. I don't want to see you end up alone out here on the plains as a miserable old hermit who's waiting to die." Fern paused to allow serenity in his voice. "I know this is sudden. I know we did not talk about it. Whether right or wrong, this is where we are at. I want you to promise me that you will give this a chance. Consider this as my gift to you because that is what it is. I mean it. Go to Yellowstone. Find yourself."

"What about you?" Noah asked. "Is this farewell?"

"No. It's an opportunity. A rare one. Once I meet these members John's talking about, I'll have options. But no matter what, I will know where you are."

"I guess I need to start packing. Do you have a plan for the ranch and the livestock? That's a lot to do by yourself."

"I'll take care of all that. You'll get your share. I'll see to it."

"I know, Fern. I've never doubted your wisdom. That's always been your gift," Noah said. He walked outside.

Fern swung the door open. "Hey!" he shouted.

Noah turned around.

"You go to Yellowstone and find that larger-than-life, guns-a-blazin' sharpshooter I once knew on the Great Plains. Forget about the past and go find your purpose."

CHAPTER 6

March 1907

Noah swung the axe dead center into the section of wood, splitting it in half. He quartered the block to fit easily in the fireplace. The cold March air gave no sign of an early spring. Snow remained deep throughout the area. High drifts formed in the dense forest from the brisk winds. The ample supply of wood provided the fuel for warmth in the quaint log cabin. Thick clouds rumbled in from the west, hinting at another round of suffocating snowfall. Noah quickened his work and chopped to replenish the woodpile and avoid another freezing night in Yellowstone National Park.

He roamed the woods in search of another dead tree for firewood. He sharpened the axe and determined the angle at which to drop the tree. A few sharp cuts made a defined wedge in the dry trunk. He reared the axe high above his head, preparing to strike the center of the tree. That was when an abrupt movement caught his attention from the tree line.

Using his peripheral vision, he steadied the axe for another swing. A dark object crept in the shadows. Noah buried the blade deep within the core. The tree shuddered from the impact. A loud crack echoed through the forest as the tree began to sway.

Noah continued cutting while glancing into the forest. A targeted hit put the tree at a slight angle. He pulled the axe away as gravity took hold. The tree smashed through the surrounding trees and crashed into the snow. Using the falling tree as a distraction, Noah seized his rifle and hid under a brush pile. He crawled through the snow and aimed into the forest, waiting for any movement to set his sights upon. He breathed slowly and prepared to fire.

He felt a tug on his right boot. Distressed at the thought of what could be behind him, he peered to see a giant gray wolf staring down at him. Noah released his rifle and dove at the wolf. The agile predator anticipated his move and attacked. Noah led with his shoulder as the wolf lunged at him, knocking Noah backward.

He collapsed in the snow and moaned from the impact as the wolf stood over him. Noah remained still while the wolf crept toward him. Noah swung his arms through the thick snow, casting it at the wolf. The alert animal leapt through the powder and landed on top of Noah, crushing him into the drift.

The wolf opened its narrow mouth and exposed its jagged fangs. Noah grabbed the wolf around its neck. Its giant paws pressed into Noah's chest, holding him against the ground. They formed a desperate embrace as the wolf snarled. With a show of dominance, it opened its mouth and dragged its wet tongue across Noah's face. The wolf shoved Noah's arms aside and began licking him with ruthless abandon.

"Ugh! Easy, Japheth. Good grief, you're heavy! Did you eat the whole deer?"

Japheth rammed Noah with his head. He turned swiftly and bit at Noah's coat sleeve. Surrendering to the incessant prodding, Noah began to scratch the wolf's belly. The fearsome predator calmed with a soothing growl.

"I've spoiled you. You are rotten," Noah said.

Japheth looked him in the eye. Noah sensed uneasiness from his formidable friend. He rubbed Japheth's long snout and scratched behind his ears. "What is it?" he asked. Japheth licked Noah again and swung around. He snarled a warning deep within his throat as Noah said, "Easy."

An Indian on horseback darted from the trees, kicking snow in every direction. The rider kept stride, barreling through drifts and branches. He halted in front of Noah and Japheth. Noah stood in front of the heaving horse. The Indian tightened the reins and positioned his horse for a rapid departure. He exuded panic as he addressed Noah.

"You need to see this," the Indian said.

"What's wrong, Kai?" Noah asked.

Kai spurred his horse and gave a terse reply. "Come now."

Noah ran to his mount, saying, "Japheth, come."

The two riders and Japheth hurried through the woods and across an open field. Kai led them a mile over the wintry terrain. The horses high-stepped through several drifts before reaching packed snow. They entered another forest and wove through the dense trees. The snow lessened, allowing them to traverse the ground with greater speed. Kai directed them to a small prairie nestled deep within the park. He stopped his mount and stayed in the saddle. Noah noticed his abrupt posture. He rode next to Kai, concerned about his odd behavior.

"What's the matter?" Noah asked.

"Look." Kai pointed ahead.

Noah gasped at the sight of six dead buffalo scattered across the blood-stained snow. Each animal was skinned of its hide and beheaded. Two calves bellowed confused cries as they wandered helplessly between the carcasses. Some of the dead buffalo had been mutilated in the pursuit of various organs. The ghastly scene humbled the men.

Japheth stepped closer to sniff the kills. "No!" Kai yelled. Japheth rushed away as Kai dismounted and approached the carcass.

He knelt near the bloody pool and rotting meat. "After the killing, they poisoned them."

Noah became uneasy. "Where are Shem and Ham?"

Noah watched Kai's appearance change as he directed him ahead of the buffalo carcasses. Noah spurred his mount with haste. Two dark objects rested near the tree line. Noah slid off the saddle and collapsed in the deep snow. He scrambled through the drift, fighting for every step, and collapsed next to one of the objects. He reached for the frozen body of a dead gray wolf.

"Shem!" he cried. A few feet away, another gray wolf had suffered the same fate. Noah yelled with growing despair, "Ham!"

Kai watched Noah hold Shem's body next to his chest and bury his face in the wolf's cold fur. Kai placed his hand on Noah's shoulder as he sobbed. The anguish of his cries brought Japheth next to him. The solemn animal sniffed his dead brother and saw his second brother covered with light snow. He joined Noah and leaned against his back with a comforting motion. Noah wrapped his arm around Japheth and cried.

Kai remained quiet in homage to the dreadful discovery. Noah laid the dead wolf on the ground and stood next to Kai.

"Japheth must have gotten away. They always hunt together." Noah looked at Japheth with confusion. "He must not have eaten any of the carcasses. But why would Shem and Ham eat the poisoned carcasses, but Japheth didn't?"

Kai knelt over Shem's body and inspected his thick fur. "Look." Kai separated the fur, exposing a small wound in the wolf's shoulder. He checked the second animal and found another wound in his neck. "They were not poisoned. They were shot." He looked back at the buffalo carcasses. "They poisoned the meat to get at Japheth. The carcasses are a trap. They kill the wolves so the wolves will not hunt the buffalo. That means more buffalo for the hunters."

"Mount up," Noah said. Both men retrieved their horses. "Which way?" Noah asked without looking at Kai.

Kai noticed some horse tracks nearby. "Those lead northeast through the valley—the easiest way out of the park."

"Get to Captain as fast as you can."

Kai looked at Noah. "Coming back to the trail will take time in this snow. How will we find you?"

"Listen for the gunshots," Noah replied.

"We must bury our dead. Don't make me bury you too."

Noah ignored Kai as rage overcame him. "Japheth, hunt!"

Japheth reacted to his master with a predator's instinct. He sniffed the ground and obtained the scent. Japheth stood four feet high at his shoulders and six feet long from his nose to the tip of his tail. The gray, brown, and tan shades of his winter coat captured the wild essence of his 110-pound body. His distinct signature of four charcoal-colored stripes contoured along his shoulders and rippled down his sides. The stripes provided a camouflage alluding to the midnight haunting of a stealthy hunter. Speed was his ally, combined with the silence of his deadly stalking. Each wolf of the three siblings had his respective traits. But for Japheth, once prey became aware of his presence, their fate was death. The lethality of his attack resembled the momentum of a charging buffalo and the striking silence of a mountain lion.

Japheth bolted through the snow with random bounds to fix his direction. The tracks appeared as horse hooves. Noah steered his mount behind Japheth, keeping the gap between them tight. What began as a narrow trail of horse tracks spread into several paths leading in the same direction. Their failure to disguise their numbers and their disregard for hiding their means of escape made it obvious that they were poachers.

Noah detested the poachers' vile and ruthless attacks. He refused to acknowledge them as people. Their selfish and lawless actions brought destruction to everything in Yellowstone. The pristine balance of nature that had existed within the park for centuries was now a fragile hope for survival. Decades of uncontrolled wildlife butchery and willful disregard for the stability of the land led to the potential annihilation of the park's animals. The cruel desire to destroy everything baffled Noah to his mental limit. The poachers had demonstrated many times before that they did not care about the future. They destroyed what Noah loved. And that made them his enemies.

Japheth stopped, and his ears perked upward. He kept a firm view ahead. Noah steered his mount into the forest and signaled for Japheth. The snow-covered wolf stood next to Noah's mount and shook the snow from his fur. Even after years of acquaintance, the composed horse displayed uneasiness around Japheth's intimidating presence.

Noah secured his horse to a tree. He checked his revolvers and loaded his rifle. Then he removed his cowboy hat and pulled a black balaclava over his head and face. Only his eyes were visible as he summoned for Japheth and traversed the trees. He kept a low profile, using the terrain and forest for cover. He advanced with a strategic intent while keeping his rifle aimed ahead and listening for the poachers' location. The element of surprise was his tactical advantage, combined with the superior strength of a massive black-striped gray wolf at his side.

The smell of a fire and the random clanking of metal led him to their campsite. Noah stared through some brush, locating eight men gathered in a circle. They worked at a fevered level, preparing the hides and packing several wagons for departure. Noah noticed that the secluded enclosure operated as a base camp for the poachers.

Two more riders arrived and joined the group. They dropped freshly skinned buffalo hides in front of the fire and hurried to flatten them across the ground. Other men performed various jobs, stripping and working the hides and heads. Noah saw dozens of hides hanging from tree limbs to dry. The entire operation was being executed with experienced precision.

Noah crawled to Japheth and said, "Stay." Japheth glared at him and growled. "No. You stay." Noah rubbed behind his ears. Japheth ignored Noah's appeasement and watched the men. Another growl rumbled deep in his throat. Noah continued rubbing and looked ahead at the poachers. "I know," he said.

Noah positioned himself near the base of a fir tree. He raised his rifle and aimed at the fire. The shot burst through the air and ripped through the middle of a coffee pot. Hot, black liquid burst around the spit, burning the surrounding men.

Noah sprinted to another tree and slid underneath the low-lying branches of a pine. Two lanterns hung on a canvas wagon. He fired two shots seconds apart. Each round slammed into the lanterns. The fuel and flame scattered across the dry canvas, igniting the cover. Fire engulfed the canvas, sending thick smoke billowing high into the air.

"There's your signal, Kai," Noah mumbled.

The poachers yelled at each other for direction. They struggled to put the fire out as the wagon began to burn. They were desperate to locate the shooter, and Noah watched the chaos develop into an organized defense. The poachers took positions under their wagons and loaded their rifles.

Noah targeted a poacher who was fleeing into the woods. He fired several shots around the runner's feet, scattering snow in small bursts. The poacher fell face-first into the snow and scampered behind a tree. Noah fired more rounds at the wagons, and the shots echoed through the woods.

The poachers became frantic, then spotted Noah. One man yelled orders to fire. Noah sprinted to the next tree. Gunshots impacted around him as the poachers fired from multiple locations. Noah remained prone and reloaded as gunshots continued to hit near him. A silence filled the area as the poachers hurried to reload.

"That should be enough," Noah whispered. He found his targets and fired three times at the wagons. He rolled behind another tree. Before the poachers could regroup, Noah fired another volley at the camp, pinning the men under the wagons. One poacher yelled a threat at Noah and aimed a buffalo gun in his direction. Noah reloaded again and aimed. He fired at the buffalo gun with a direct hit. The weapon flew out of the poacher's hands. The man bellowed in pain, holding his bloodied arm.

"They shot me!" the poacher yelled. "They're trying to kill us!"

"You killed my wolves!" Noah responded.

Numerous gunshots littered the ground near Noah. He watched as the poachers dispersed in teams. He fired at the wagons again. Another silence occurred as the poachers returned no gunfire. Noah looked at the camp as the distinct click of a revolver sounded from behind him.

"Drop that rifle!"

Noah saw one of the poachers aiming at him.

"I mean it!" the man said.

Several more poachers ran from the campsite. Noah released his weapon and stayed on the ground.

"Get up. Where are the others? You can't be alone." The poacher stepped from behind a tree and approached Noah. "He's over here!" he called.

Noah watched the poacher come closer, slowly placed two fingers between his teeth, and whistled.

Grrr . . .

The poacher's eyes widened at the sound of a sinister growl behind him. As he turned around, Japheth leapt through the air and slammed into him. The wolf locked his fangs deep into the falling man's shoulder. Japheth tore into him with a fiendish frenzy. He ripped the coat and shirt off the man and tore the skin and hair from his body. The poacher screamed from the attack. He raised his revolver at Japheth, but the furious animal clamped down on the man's wrist with a voracious bite. Bones snapped and popped from the immense pressure as Japheth swung his head back and forth in a vicious rage.

"Japheth, come!" Noah ordered.

The enraged wolf released the mauled man, whose useless hand dangled by shredded tendons as he moaned in the snow. Noah saw four poachers aim at Japheth. He reached for his revolver and cocked the hammer. An arrow streaked by his line of sight and penetrated a poacher. The man fell with the arrow protruding from his forearm. The other poachers halted their advance and searched the woods for the shooter.

Kai stepped from a tree and released another arrow at one of the men. The razor-sharp flint found its target in a poacher's leg. One man noticed Kai and raised his rifle to return fire. But he stepped backward as fifteen mounted soldiers raced past Kai. The speed of the cavalry overwhelmed the poachers. The soldiers encircled the group with guns drawn and forced a desperate surrender.

Noah directed Japheth away from the soldiers. They made several arrests and prepared the poachers for transport. Noah walked the campsite, watching the event unfold. Soldiers documented the evidence of the buffalo kills and questioned the poachers. Noah felt satisfaction from the encounter, but he remained angry over the loss of his wolves. Having to stand near the guilty parties began to infuriate him. His discipline to avoid the poachers and not finish the fight began to wane. Kai saw Noah seething at the poachers. Noah placed his hand on his revolver.

Whoosh!

Noah jumped as an arrow wisped through the air and impacted a tree next to him. He saw Kai lower his bow. Furious, he ripped the arrow from the bark and stormed after Kai. The calm Shoshone stood still as Noah advanced. Kai raised an eyebrow in subtle warning. Seeing his resilience, Noah regained composure.

"It took you long enough," Noah said as he handed Kai the arrow.

"I was hungry. Stopped by the cabin for a sandwich."

Noah surrendered to laughter. "That's funny because I know you don't lie. Thank you, my friend. You kept death away from me."

"Again," Kai said.

"Was that enough shots fired for you to find us?" Noah asked. "Those fools had no idea they were signaling the US Army."

"Just like the rest. No sense. Only destruction," Kai said.

"Yes, their own," Noah replied. He strolled to the wagons and perused the poachers' items. Several buffalo hides, heads, and weaponry were scattered over the rigs. Noah saw a large chest and kicked it open. Whiskey bottles, ammunition, and cutting utensils were piled inside. He shifted the items around, revealing a leather bag at the bottom of the chest. He pulled the tie loose and opened the bag. Pounds of coins, gold, and silver pieces clinked in the bag. Using both hands, he pulled the heavy bag from the chest and wrapped it in a patchwork quilt. He twisted the quilt and heaved it over his shoulder.

"Wolf!"

Noah saw several soldiers surrounding Japheth. They aimed their rifles and yelled for permission to shoot. "That thing is huge! Watch out!" a soldier warned.

A cavalry sergeant rode next to the panicked group. "Why isn't it running away?" he asked. "Put it down before it attacks someone."

"That wolf is mine!" Noah pushed through the soldiers and stood next to Japheth. He rubbed behind his ears. "Anyone with sense can see he won't hurt your soldiers," he said.

"I don't care who that thing belongs to. That wolf should not be on park grounds." He ordered two of his soldiers. "Both of you, ready your rifles." He confronted Noah again. "Mister, I suggest you step aside."

Japheth growled in contempt as Noah remained. "My wolf doesn't like stupid people."

The sergeant gave him a defiant look and told his men, "Take aim . . ."

Noah pulled his revolver and aimed at the sergeant. "I don't like stupid people either."

"That's enough!" A captain rode into the group and waved off the men. "Lower your weapons! Sergeant, get a detail and check the perimeter. I want every bit of evidence found." He focused on four other soldiers. "You men, confiscate these wagons and get them secured. I want everything ready to move in one hour."

The men hurried away as the captain rode next to Noah. "I see that your demeanor toward humanity remains consistent," the captain said with a condescending tone. "I must say, I am impressed. Yet another temptation to breach your contract and kill every one of these vermin. If there is anyone who could have done it alone, it would have been you." The captain surveyed the area. "How many have we caught this week? I'm guessing about twenty?"

Noah holstered his revolver. "Closer to thirty." He looked at the poachers being handcuffed and loaded in the wagons. "I recognize that bunch. They have been caught before."

"That's what I was afraid of. I'll inform command. We will keep demanding tougher sentencing."

"For what?" Noah responded. "To release them a day later? Look around you, Captain Hendricks. This isn't working. You hardly have any buffalo left in the entire park. If it weren't for the guard around the Mammoth area, Yellowstone wouldn't have any buffalo at all."

"It takes time to enforce regulations, and, as you know, we have a lot of park to cover," Captain Joseph Hendricks replied. He looked at Japheth and studied the menacing wolf. "I got a report the other day that three gray wolves were spotted southwest of here. One fit the description of that one right there." Noah remained quiet as Captain Hendricks continued. "I thought we had an agreement. You know wolves should not be on park grounds anyway. You cannot fight that in court."

"Has any progress been made on changing the law for predators yet?" Noah asked.

"That's not under my influence, Noah. You know that. No predators on protected lands. We must keep them out of the park."

"By exterminating them?" Noah asked.

"The regulations are to protect the buffalo. Until legislation occurs otherwise, you keep your word."

"What report?" Noah asked. He confronted Captain Hendricks with rising anger. "Joseph, you don't know if your men saw wolves, coyotes, or a pack of prairie dogs."

The captain looked around for anyone listening. "You know what I'm talking about! I can't protect you if you don't meet me halfway. Quit acting like this is your park. It's not." He paused as Kai stopped his mount next to them. "It's bad enough having to deal with these wretched poachers every day. I don't need another headache from you. I know what you and Kai are trying to do here. It's admirable, I'll give you that. But the politicians don't see it that way. You keep out of sight, or you will force me to take action."

"Action? Kai and I found two dead wolves not far from several poisoned buffalo carcasses. They were my wolves. And they shot them!" Noah watched the shackled poachers leaving on the wagons.

Captain Hendricks ordered his remaining soldiers to leave. "I have patrols working all over the park. Poachers are getting bolder and more desperate. We are doing what we can with what we have."

"It's not enough. This policy is weak. You and your men can't control this park. If you could, my wolves would be alive." Noah became furious. "It's your failure that killed them and those buffalo."

"Watch yourself, Noah. I know you are angry about your wolves, but your accusations could make things complicated. For both of us."

"Complicated?" Noah sneered. "I thought we had an agreement. Remember what you just said to me?"

"I think you need to leave," Captain Hendricks replied.

"Meet me halfway. Do you remember saying that too? Is that what we have, Joseph? Are we meeting each other halfway?" Noah asked.

"You fulfill your contract. Anything else is unchanged. How you want to interpret that is up to you. Don't make me the enemy." Captain Hendricks faced Kai. "Good work today, Kai. You're still the best tracker I know. You make us and the Tukudika people proud." He paused to emphasize his words. "Have you thought any more about my job offer?"

"Leave him alone," Noah interrupted.

"We talked about this before, Noah. Having Kai train army scouts would benefit all of us. With more experienced men, we could cover more ground and better protect the Henrys Lake area and the park's western border. Besides, I think it's Kai's decision to make," Captain Hendricks said.

Kai looked at Noah and did not hesitate. "I think I'll stay here, Captain."

Captain Hendricks gave a disgruntled reply. "I can't say I see the attraction. These contract jobs you two have won't last forever. I'm offering you steady work with army pay. But you can't blame me for trying." He positioned his horse to leave and faced Noah a final time. "It looks like snow is coming. It's been a long winter. Longer than I remember." Noah remained unmoved as Captain Hendricks continued. "I'm sorry about your wolves." He spurred his mount and rode away.

Kai watched him depart and asked, "Is the captain angry?"

Noah watched the snow blow in a fine mist from a distant mountain peak. The air chilled as a winter front drifted through the trees. He thought of Captain Hendricks' words and contemplated his situation. Frustrated with the political quagmire and saddened at the loss of his wolves, he knew Captain Hendricks was not to blame. The constant fight against poachers and the burden of regulations that prevented improvement repressed his resolve. He considered Captain Hendricks a trusted friend and knew he would forgive him. As he watched the weather deteriorate into a snowstorm, he pondered how he would forgive himself.

He looked away from the view and addressed Kai. "No. He is covering his backside." Noah hesitated in continued thought. "I think we need to move our operation farther into the mountains. Until the politicians in the East make laws to protect all the wildlife, we need to stay hidden."

"You cannot hide the wildlife," Kai said. "This is their home."

"That's true. And no one knows that better than you. But I don't have an answer to this, and Captain Hendricks is too overwhelmed to help us. We must do what we can to prevent what happened to Shem and Ham from happening again."

Kai observed the valley. "I knew this land when it was wild. A land where the mighty roamed." He faced Noah with pride. "A land where my people roamed. Now there is none."

"You are my friend. I believe in you. With you, we have hope. I don't want our work of many years moved to the reservation. For even that may not be an option for us. These animals, this park, and even this land depend upon us. You keep believing in what we are doing. In time, those in the East will see the error of their ways. Just as I did." Noah returned to the mountain view. "Let's move what animals we have to the snow line cabin. We will build the preserve farther away from the valleys. Once we get established, we can decide what to do from there. At least the animals can roam safely and away from poachers. They won't hunt above the snow line."

"It is harder to protect the animals. They keep getting killed. If not Yellowstone, where would we go? We may be on our own," Kai replied.

Noah placed his hand on Kai's shoulder. "That's what scares me."

September 1907

The late summer warmth blended with the coolness of altitude. The mountain slope, with its green swaths of prairies and dense border forests, provided an ample play area. Noah and Kai watched from the trees as four rambunctious wolf pups rolled in the grass. The she-wolf lounged nearby, enjoying a break from the energetic party. The pups lunged and barked at each other with carefree joy. The passing clouds accentuated the blue horizon, presenting a mountainous view that spanned Yellowstone Park. Remnant snowbanks glistened in the sunlight. The drifts resembled island chains scattered across the rocky snow line. As Noah and Kai took in the tranquil scene, the optimism of new life brought harmony to the pristine landscape.

They returned to their horses and traversed the woods back to their cabin. The remote location provided safety for the fragile species of wildlife under their care. Predators and occasional wounded animals received treatment and protection under the men's watchful presence. Their secluded retreat provided several corrals and a barn for every animal requiring reprieve from the assault of valley poachers and bordering ranchers. Despite the obstacles, their sanctuary offered devotion and determination to the striving wildlife of Yellowstone.

They exited the forest to see their cabin nestled on a plateau bordering several pastures protected by pines. A wisp of smoke rose from the stone chimney, which never saw reprieve from fire. Two deer fed along the south side of the cabin. They raised their heads in alarm, only to return to their feasting at the sight of Noah and Kai. Squirrels gave chase in the limbs. Horses, cattle, and several bighorn sheep complemented the setting from within the corral. The rustic oasis of wildlife and nature welcomed them home.

"We have a visitor," Kai said. They noticed a man sitting near the cabin door.

Noah squinted through the sunlight. "That looks like John Bruce." Kai angled his horse away. "Where are you going?"

Kai responded without looking at Noah. "He always wants something. It is better if I go."

"Maybe I should go too," he mumbled. But he continued toward the cabin and offered the first greeting. "Am I fired?"

"I haven't seen you in two years, and that is your welcome?" John asked.

"I figured Captain Hendricks would be contacting you before long," Noah said. "What version of the truth got relayed to you this time?"

"What are you talking about? Captain Hendricks is one of our most trusted advisors." He paused in gradual realization. "Uh-oh. What have you done now?"

Noah told John about the death of his wolves and the ongoing problem with poachers. John listened, observing the distress in Noah's demeanor. Noah finished his story and portrayed disgust at having to relive the painful memory.

John tried to console him, saying, "I'm more confident than ever that laws will be passed to protect the wolves in Yellowstone."

"Laws only protect them on paper. You know any laws out here must be enforced," Noah said. "It's urgent. There is too much against them." Noah unsaddled his horse and led John into the cabin. He stoked the fire and offered a coffee.

They reclined near the fireplace as John continued their conversation. "I know you and Kai have achieved great success with your sanctuary. Wolves have a fighting chance and a place of refuge. This has worked well, and the other wildlife numbers are stable."

"But far from recovered. You know what we are up against," Noah said.

"Yes, but imagine where Yellowstone would be without your work. You and Kai deserve the credit for what I have seen grow and flourish here, regardless of numbers." John set his coffee aside. "Which is why I am here."

Noah chuckled. "Let me guess. You want something?"

John stretched his legs across the hearth. "Close. Someone wants *you*."

"What?" Noah asked.

"You have been requested," John said. Noah raised his eyebrows as he continued. "You and your unique services have been requested to start a new sanctuary very soon. It is a wildlife preserve very similar to what you have here but at a more intensified scale."

"More than Yellowstone?" Noah asked. "What wildlife is involved?"

"There is a plan for the buffalo to return there. It is quite political and very high-profile," John replied.

"No," Noah said. "Not interested."

"I haven't told you the full extent of the plan."

"You don't need to. It is not working at Yellowstone. The buffalo continue to die from poachers, the army is still struggling to establish a foothold within the park, and your politicians do nothing to stop the real problems that prevent us from progressing." Noah stared into the fire, "I am not able to protect them."

"I understand your concern, but this request is asking for you by name. And I am too. We need you to go observe the situation, perform as an advisor, and provide a supportive role to the effort there. We are building something new by starting a preserve from the beginning. As for you, I need you to look at this as an opportunity to share any lessons learned from your work at Yellowstone. Both the good and the not so good." Moments passed in silence. "You must understand. We need you, Noah. This is what I recruited you for. We do not have very many converted buffalo hunters willing or able to run wildlife sanctuaries in remote places."

"Who are you fooling? You don't have any!" Both men smiled. "So, where is this place?"

John perked at the encouragement. "It's an area you may be familiar with, from what you have mentioned to me before. It's a forest and game preserve in southwest Oklahoma Territory." Noah remained quiet. "I have a contact there who will provide you with more details when you arrive." John sat up in his chair. "And before you say anything, there is a very attractive financial incentive for you when you get there. Consider it a retention bonus for your loyalty and continued service to the society."

"You would make a great politician."

John ignored his condescending remark. "The arrival of the buffalo to this preserve is the priority. They must be placed in a protected environment. Can we count on you to help us with that?"

Noah watched the flames flicker over the coals. He looked around the cabin interior as he contemplated the offer. His mind searched for solace as his heart warned of fervor. What he lived daily had suddenly become more than he'd realized with John's words. The sanctuary fulfilled a means to a purpose. But it also had become his home. As he adored the comfort of the log-lined walls, he looked at John and agreed reluctantly.

Noah fastened his saddlebags and secured the remaining items to the mount. Kai held the reins as Noah extended his hand and said, "I will see you again. Work with your Shoshone brothers. In case you need to move the sanctuary, have them help." Kai agreed and pointed behind Noah. Japheth waited with curiosity.

Noah knelt next to him. Japheth jumped at the reception and nudged Noah with affection. "You aren't making this easy," Noah said. He rubbed Japheth behind the ears. "You are safer here. I will come back." He leaned closer to Japheth and whispered, "You are my wolf, my Japheth." He hugged Japheth with constrained sadness. The wolf lunged forward, pawing at Noah. His ears perked in the direction of the forest as a man on horseback emerged from the trees.

"Captain," Kai stated.

Captain Hendricks dismounted. "I heard from a reliable source that you are leaving us."

"John has a big mouth," Noah said.

Captain Hendricks chuckled. "I'm sure you will give ol' Kai a much-needed break." They sat on large sections of wood. "I think it is noble what you are doing. These new preserves need all the help they can get. Getting one started is half the battle. Keeping it going is the other."

"Knowing John, I expect some pain awaits," Noah replied.

"I'm sure it does."

"I find it hard to believe you rode up here just to send me off. There must be another problem."

"Unfortunately, yes. Those poachers we arrested a while back keep filing charges about their money that went missing. From what they say, it was a very large amount. It happened during that scuffle they had with you before we showed up. They said it had nothing to do with their poaching. They are making a real stink about it, and I must investigate."

"They killed my wolves and butchered our buffalo. All on park land. Did anyone make a stink about that?"

"I didn't come up here for another lesson, Noah."

"Then maybe they should have paid more attention to their money instead of trying to kill me!" He looked Captain Hendricks in the eyes. "I should have shot them all when there were no witnesses. It would have been better for everybody. Then you would have something real to investigate instead of a bunch of poachers and attempted murderers crying about their missing money."

"With or without a contract, you are too good a man for that. It would be a waste anyway," Captain Hendricks replied. "Their day is coming. We are winning. It's a big park with a lot of ground to cover." He stared at Noah. "You have put up with a lot. And lost a lot. I know how you are about your wolves." He looked at Japheth, who was lying next to Noah. "I guess in a perfect world, those poachers would owe you compensation for what they have done to you."

Noah rubbed Japheth behind the ears. "They would in an imperfect world too."

Captain Hendricks watched Japheth look at Noah. The visible bond between them enticed envy. "Amazing. Well, I see no need in chasing a dead end. I consider this investigation closed." He addressed Kai. "Kai, if you will second that proposal, I think I will let you gentlemen enjoy the rest of your day." He stood and mounted his horse.

Kai went inside the cabin as Noah approached Captain Hendricks. He handed him the reins and said, "I owe you an apology." Captain Hendricks was surprised. "You have always been a good friend to me, Joseph. You are someone I trust. And trust is hard to come by." He tossed Captain Hendricks a leather bag. "This is from me to you, as a friend, not an army officer. I know you and your morals are too stubborn to take it from me otherwise." Captain

Hendricks stared at the bag. "There is over $1,000 in that," Noah said.

Captain Hendricks leaned his head back and asked, "Do I want to know?"

"That is my money. Retribution for my two wolves, Shem and Ham, which those heathens took from me," Noah said. "That money is for you and your family. Use it." Captain Hendricks remained quiet. "Kai is overseeing the operation while I'm gone. I would be grateful if you would check in on him every now and then, as a friend."

"I'd be honored." The captain secured the bag and looked down at Noah. A sense of regret resonated in his voice. "If I didn't have obligations, I would join you both."

"I've never said this to anyone, but I was wrong. I should not have said those things to you at the poachers' campsite that day. You're a good man. Thank you for having my back when no one had yours," Noah said.

"Make sure you watch that temper of yours. Those folks down in Oklahoma Territory may not be as forgiving as I am."

"That's a work in progress," Noah jeered.

"We can only do what we are capable of and what the moment allows." Captain Hendricks prepared to depart.

"At what risk?" Noah asked, deliberately enticing him.

"Wrong question!" Captain Hendricks yelled at a gallop.

Noah cupped his hands around his mouth and hollered, "How's that?"

Captain Hendricks stopped his horse. "Everything has a risk, my friend. But for people like us, the question is, *At what choice?*" He saluted Noah, then spurred his horse through the trees.

CHAPTER 7

September 1907

Rebecca McGovern watched from outside the fence that enclosed a small meadow. Overhanging limbs shaded her favorite spot for observing through the high-wired enclosure. Trees and shrubs surrounded the grass lot, providing a natural contrast to the artificial barrier. A morning breeze stirred the inhabitants from their slumber. She waited eagerly for a response to her call. The rising sun pierced the leafy canopy. Warm summer rays highlighted the first of several buffalo meandering toward Rebecca from within the New York Zoological Park.

She recognized each buffalo and offered fresh grass through the fencing. As she coaxed them forward, a few of the hungry beasts ripped the grass from the fencing and chewed in front of her. She tossed little piles of grass over the fence, attracting more of them. She spoke to each one with tender encouragement. The buffalo devoured the grass and sniffed for more. Rebecca offered the last bale and continued admiring them.

The outer gate slammed shut as John Bruce stopped next to her. He surveyed the docile scene. The buffalo gathered in front of him, expecting more grass. He watched their demanding appearance. Their time in captivity had obvious influence on their demeanor, but he knew the animals remained wild at heart. He yearned to share the hope for that wildness in the land of their ancestors.

"Hi Dad. Beautiful, aren't they," Rebecca said.

"Yes, they are," John responded as he hugged his daughter.

"Do you think this will work?" Rebecca asked with her eyes fixed on the herd.

"All the arrangements have been made. It is our oversight that will answer your question."

"We worked so hard to get them here," Rebecca said.

"We are only sending fifteen of them for reintroduction. It's a conservative approach."

"I don't like the risk. They must travel a long way, and so many things could go wrong." Rebecca paused. "So many things already have. I think of the sacrifices that have been made, even long ago."

John spoke with solemn appeal. "Your husband's sacrifice has not been forgotten. Andrew's contribution and passing those many years ago are why we must continue our efforts. He will always be an inspiration for me. He is why I continue to fight for our cause. What I would have given to have had his influence in Washington. He would have been a monumental factor for the cause. It pains me to think of the happiness the two of you could have had together. I miss him."

"I know. I do too. Every moment of every day. Either way, the risk for these animals makes me very uncomfortable," Rebecca said.

"Risk is why we are here. It is our role to mitigate the risk as much as possible." John looked at the buffalo as they wandered the enclosure, and he knew the moment was at hand. He spoke with authority, but Rebecca detected the reservation in his words. "Which is why I am sending you out there now."

"Now? I was hoping to go with the main party and help with the rail transport."

"Transportation does not require our involvement. There are others more than capable of handling that part of the plan," John said. "Our role is to ensure the location is ready to receive the buffalo."

Rebecca heard the concern in his voice. "We all know that. Most of the planning has been focused on the location since the beginning. What's wrong? Is it the tick problem again? I know they are worried about the danger of transmitting the fever when the buffalo arrive."

"No. The staff are performing controlled pasture burns and working other pest remedies to minimize that risk," he replied. "It's the senior members of the society. I met with them, and we discussed several topics. They are concerned about the predator problem. In particular, the gray wolves. They consider them a long-term threat to the entire project."

"What did they say about the predator drives? We can focus the same effort on the wolves and drive them off the preserve," Rebecca said.

"They want immediate success, and the predator drives take time." John became agitated. "Then the problem becomes what to do with the wolves once they are driven off the preserve. Even in a place that remote, the preserve has become more contained by the surrounding cattle ranchers and farmers. Even the military has a presence there."

"What happened with the predator relocation discussion? We can do that for the wolves too," she said.

"You are an animal biologist, Becky. You, of all people, should know the temperament of a wild gray wolf! This isn't some outdated cattle drive with a derelict bull leading a herd down the dusty trail. Frankly, you are going to what is left of the Wild West."

"Relocation was your idea!" Rebecca countered.

"Yes, I know."

"Then do it!" she shouted.

"It is not that simple!"

"What has gotten you so upset?"

John leaned against the fence. Rebecca reached for his arm as he said, "It has become political. The senior members did not like what

I had to say. They took over the predator relocation plan. I'm waiting for their decision. We will proceed once we have it."

"Okay. So, you don't have control of the plan. I know that bothers you. But once we get something, we will be fine," she stated.

"The senior members do not know that area. It isn't Yellowstone National Park, where you have the Rocky Mountains to hide in," John replied.

"We wait and see what they come up with and continue planning until then."

John shook his head with animosity. "In all our projects, I have never seen them this apprehensive before."

"Look, with the predator drives, we can do this humanely. We relocate them and benefit everyone. Especially the wildlife. The senior members know this," she said.

John was reluctant to speak the truth as he became firm with his responses. "They want a guarantee that there will be no wolves on the preserve when the buffalo arrive in October."

"Fine," Rebecca answered. "We will get the plan and organize when I get out there."

"It's September! Any time for organizing is against us." John sighed. "I am concerned for where this might lead."

Rebecca became defensive. "Hunts are out of the question! The locals there are already killing them at random. Please tell me that is not an option."

"I made it clear we are not employing extirpative measures."

"There is something fundamentally wrong about interfering with the natural order of a species. But I must admit, for a predator drive on a preserve that big, I'm not sure I know where to start," Rebecca said.

"Which is why I sent another contact there to assist you." John's reluctance was obvious as he continued. "Sometimes, I must do what is needed, so this is somewhat off the books. When you get there, I ask that you keep his presence discreet."

"A secret? You really are having trust issues with the senior members, aren't you?"

"I'm sending him there to help you."

"Oh, so now I need help, and I'm not even there yet. Wonderful. Your lack of confidence in this is beginning to show. Or is it with me?"

"No, never."

"Good. Please don't regard me with your distaste for the senior members." She allowed a momentary silence to diffuse the stalled discussion. "So, who is this phantom contact?"

"He is unrefined, but he has the experience we need." John looked at her with a father's love. "My hope is that he will provide options for you should your exceptional skills ever need them."

Rebecca presented a wide smile. "That's better. Can we trust him?"

"I've known him a long time, and I've seen him work. I kept him remote for several years on a trial project. He is headstrong but devoted." John became engrossed in thought.

"What?" she asked.

"It's more of an interest than a concern. This man seems to have an ability. It is as if he can communicate with wildlife—wolves in particular. I've only seen it once, but I have to admit it is rather fascinating to witness."

"Great. At night, does he go outside and howl at the moon?"

"Very funny," John said. "Whatever abilities he has may be of service to us. If things should become complicated, don't count him out."

"And if things should get out of control, what then?"

John raised his eyebrows. "Whoever is on the receiving end of that man's wrath had better hope *he* doesn't get out of control."

"Well then, I'll be extra careful," Rebecca said.

"You already know my contact stationed there."

"Two contacts are better than none. It's a start and will save us time."

"Actually, the senior members are placing a third contact directly with the staff to work on the preserve. He will assist you with the effort on-site, but he reports to the senior members, not me. They want him informed of everything so the preserve staff are aware as they prepare for the buffalo's arrival," John said. "I have all the information and contact names in a folder for you. You will have plenty to review on your trip west.

Rebecca focused on the buffalo herd. "It is disheartening how complicated this has become. Looking at them is to look at history. At a simpler time. They are so strong but now so fragile in number."

"They are survivors, and they need our help," John said. "They were never meant to be caged or put in a zoo. They are meant to roam." He faced Rebecca. "We have never had this level of scrutiny of our work. Our success will solidify our position among the elites in Washington for future projects. They are expecting results that we must provide. Again, these buffalo must arrive at a protected environment. We do not have much time."

"They have been through so much and have come so far," she said. "And now they are going on another long journey."

John put his arm around Rebecca and admired the herd. "They are going home."

Noah dismounted and stretched his aching back. He tied his horse to the post and faced the ranch house door. Taking a moment, he walked to the middle of the yard. He closed his eyes and cleared his mind. Calming from the tiresome journey, he opened his eyes.

The surrounding prairie stretched for miles in every direction. The dry heat and steady wind brushed by his face. He took a deep breath and sensed the forgotten smell of dried sage grass. The musty aroma invigorated his memory. The feeling that the elements provided him revived his dormant past. His soul awakened with the recollection of his previous life on the Great Plains.

Rolling hills to the north met mountains of granite leading westward. Mesquite trees were scattered over the few remaining unplowed fields. The southern view appeared limitless, extending over open grasslands to the Texas border. As he stood in the southwestern scene, early memories were rejuvenated. He felt his soul awaken from the years spent away. The moment resurrected the lost tranquility of the land he truly loved. With the sun on his face and the long wait finally over, his return to Oklahoma Territory felt like more than a journey ended. It felt like home.

"You stand there much longer, and folks will think you're a scarecrow!" a woman yelled from the cabin door.

Noah hurried to the front porch. "Hello, ma'am. I'm Noah Wrath. I was told to come to this address by a Mister John Bruce."

"We've been expecting you, Noah. Welcome to Cache. My name is Cecilia. Come inside from that wretched sun. You must be parched from riding in that miserable heat."

"It has been a while since I've been in heat like this. As crazy as it sounds, I miss it," Noah replied.

"Yes, I would say that is crazy." Cecilia ushered him in to sit at the table. "How was your trip? You came all the way from Wyoming, am I right?"

"Yes, ma'am. The Great Plains have changed since the last time I traveled through them. I didn't think I would ever get here."

The front door swung open. A man entered the cabin with two people following and yelled at Noah, "Whose smelly horse is that outside?"

Noah's eyes widened with sudden recognition. "Fern!" He pushed the chair away and bounded across the room. The two men met with a firm embrace. "I can't believe it's you. What are you doing here?"

"This is our ranch," Fern replied. He stepped aside and introduced the people behind him. "Noah, I'd like you to meet Mrs. Dee Cassidy and her husband, Louis Cassidy, the sheriff of Cache."

Noah greeted the couple. "John Bruce didn't say anything about—"

"Me?" Fern asked. "I know. I told him not to. I didn't think you would come all this way if you knew it was me requesting you."

"Why would you think that?"

"I was afraid there might be some hard feelings. It wasn't the best of times when we left each other in Montana."

Noah embraced Fern again. "There is no such thing. I've missed you. More than you know."

"I've missed you too. I don't want to know how many years it has been. Seems life decided to stampede on us right about the time we thought we had it figured out," Fern said. He looked at Cecilia with an anxious grin. "Have you been properly introduced yet? Does he know?"

Cecilia rolled her eyes and said, "Go on, have your moment."

Fern laughed with hearty eagerness and presented as though he was making a speech. "Cecilia, this is the greatest scout, hunter, gunslinger, horseman, and friend I know."

"That's quite a list, Noah," Cecilia said.

"Yes, ma'am," Noah replied. "And most of them are lies. My hope is that he will run out of breath."

"Hey!" Fern extended his arms. "And Noah, this is Cecilia." He hugged her.

"I think I'm ahead of you on this one, ol' buddy."

"Cecilia Raul, my wife."

"Uh, wife?"

Fern bellowed with laughter. "Yes! Cecilia is another reason I wanted you to come. I wanted you to meet my best friend and the love of my life."

Noah addressed Cecilia. "I never thought any woman could tame this bronco. Well, there certainly is no questioning your courage, Mrs. Raul."

"He's good to have around when the fences need mending. And call me Cecilia. We are happy to have you, Noah."

Fern kissed her cheek and looked at Noah. "You must be hungry. We have much to talk about."

They gathered around the table for a welcomed feast. Noah and Fern reminisced about their time together. The inflated stories by one led to contradictions by the other. They spoke of their time apart with curiosity and interest. Apologies were attempted and denied as unnecessary. The years spent apart were quickly erased as both men reinvigorated their lasting bond. Cecilia questioned every comment for validity and enjoyed the abounding humor at each man's expense. Hours passed as the dormant friendship livened with maturity and strength.

"Noah, what Fernando has failed to mention is the connection between these two women," Sheriff Cassidy said, alluding to Cecilia and his wife. "I think you should be fairly warned."

"Watch yourself, Sheriff," Dee said with a grin.

Fern chimed in. "What the good sheriff is trying to say is that these two are sisters. And as feisty as they come too."

"That is hardly the case, Noah," Dee responded. "As long as this bunch does what I say, life is good."

Cecilia interrupted. "Stop spreading lies to him. He hasn't been here a day, and already you are ordering folks around."

"Don't get these two started, Noah," Sheriff Cassidy advised. "They are ruthless. Cecilia, tell Noah what you used to do to my poor wife when you two were younger."

"And you are telling *him* not to get us started?" Dee asked and threw her napkin at Louis. "Cecilia, don't you dare!"

Cecilia leaned against the table. "It was completely harmless. Anytime my sister decided to order me around, I would get my fill and lock her in the closet. I know I felt better afterward."

"You were mean. You still are," Dee said.

"Although her screaming did get old after an hour or so," Cecilia jeered.

"Do you see, Noah? I warned you," Louis added.

"Enough, you two," Fern said. "You will have him on the next train out of Cache at this rate!" He directed his attention to Noah. "I'm surprised you didn't bring your wolf. John said it rarely leaves your side."

"I debated it. It was hard to leave him. His name is Japheth. I raised him and his two brothers from pups."

"Japheth? And what are the names of the other two?"

Noah knew Fern was provoking him. "Shem and Ham."

"Right out of Genesis! Very creative. A bit odd, but at least you don't take yourself too seriously. How did you end up with three gray wolves?"

"They were strays. I found them when their mother was shot by poachers. Japheth is the last of the pack." Noah avoided eye contact.

Fern noticed his change in demeanor. The light tone of their conversation subsided to seriousness. "I know the army has its hands full protecting a place as vast and rugged as Yellowstone. I'm sure the politics get in the way too."

"Just how much do you know about Yellowstone?" Noah asked.

"I checked with John every now and then. I wanted to make sure you weren't losing that temper of yours and getting in too much trouble," Fern replied. "Is the buffalo population still struggling up there?"

"We are adding to the herd, but the poachers and the politicians still get in the way of progress. We started a wildlife sanctuary for predators and strays years ago. We are doing what we can."

"John told me you achieved some success. You know, he speaks highly of you."

"I wouldn't know about that, from either of you."

Fern was surprised by his comment. But rather than react and risk the enjoyment of the evening, he allowed his previous influence over Noah to flourish again.

"Noah, my leaving was never meant to hurt our friendship. We needed time to figure ourselves out. I know I did." Fern spoke with genuine fervor. "All considered, how have you been?"

Noah hesitated, debating the direction of their discussion. "I like the seclusion. I have a good friend there named Kai. He is Shoshone and the best scout I've ever seen. He reminds me a lot of you, but with fewer words."

Fern said, "Obviously, he is a fine man."

"Now you've done it, Noah," Cecilia said. "It's beginning to get deep in here." She giggled at Fern and took their plates from the table. "You let me know if you need anything."

"Thank you for a wonderful meal," Noah said. "I haven't eaten like that in, well, ever."

Sheriff Cassidy and Dee expressed their pleasantries and followed Cecilia away from the table. Fern blew a kiss at Cecilia and looked at Noah. "What about the last thing we talked about before you left for Yellowstone? Did you find a purpose?"

Noah chose his response with reservation. "I found a reason." He thought of Yellowstone. "It is a hard living there, and cold. But it gives a reason to the day when I can help the wildlife. I feel like I've corrected some of what we did hunting buffalo all those years."

"I'm glad to hear that," Fern replied. "Because that is exactly why I requested for you to come here."

Noah became intrigued. "John said something about starting a wildlife preserve and bringing in some buffalo."

"Yes. It is very exciting," Fern said. "All of Oklahoma Territory is talking about it. Some other folks John knows are transporting fifteen buffalo by rail from a zoo in New York to the Wichita Mountains. President Roosevelt himself started this wildlife preserve. The buffalo will have dedicated protection, overseers, and everything they need to establish a herd."

"Sounds simple enough," Noah said.

"Hardly. With you here, this is no longer focused solely on fifteen buffalo returning to the Great Plains. There is another agenda that is not very outspoken and rather difficult to approach. For years now, no one has been able to solve the predator problem."

"Predator problem?" Noah chuckled. "That can be a contradiction in terms. It depends on defining the predator. Where I'm from, our predator problem has two legs, not four. How does this involve me?"

"By doing exactly what you've done at Yellowstone. We need you to save the wildlife that is native to this area. What is left of them."

"Do you know what it means to start something like this? It is much more than a one-person job, and every location is different. What works at one place may not at another."

"Perhaps," Fern said. "But we didn't know it was this bad. The predator population here is nearly extinct. Bears, mountain lions, bobcats, and many more have suffered great losses. The concern is for the wolves. The gray wolves in particular."

"It's the same problem at Yellowstone. If the wildlife is not on some politically protected list, the chances of saving them are slim. The government, ranchers, and farmers encourage the hunting of the gray wolf. If that is the case here, I don't know how I can help," Noah said.

"I think your work and success with that wolf of yours back at Yellowstone proves otherwise."

"Oh, come on, Fern! You know as well as I do that wolves are not pets. This isn't some dog kennel in the middle of a city that we're talking about. These are wild animals and not to be underestimated. I raised Japheth from a pup and worked with him every day. He is different. Taking a fully grown and mature gray wolf out of the wild and training against that instinct is impossible. I lost my other two wolves to poachers. I trained them to stay away from people, and they still ended up dead in one of the most remote places in the country. I asked you if you know what it means to start something like this. It can be more than the work that is needed. It can be a sacrifice that leads to a painful loss."

Fern felt Noah's words and thought of a careful response. "I can appreciate all you have been through, and I am sorry for the loss of your wolves. I know what they meant to you. But that is exactly why you are here. We need your help—help only you can provide. I don't know of anyone else with your experience and desire for something like this. It is unique. I don't mean to use my words against you, but I asked you a long time ago to find your purpose. What else would have more purpose for you than this?" Fern let his words resonate, then continued. "And aside from how we may feel about any of this, we are getting paid for something that is much larger than us. I need you to keep in mind that John has his expectations. Tomorrow, I'll take you to the preserve to meet the staff. We can discuss it further with them."

"Unless they have answers I've never seen before, I still don't know how to help," Noah replied. "I'm sorry too."

"Give us tomorrow. Then I think you will know what to do. Enough for tonight. Let's get you bedded down in your room. I've got a stall in the barn for your horse."

"Fern," Noah said, staring at the table. "Is there anyone around here you can trust? I can tell you from experience, it all starts and ends with that."

"There are some good folks on the preserve. But, like anywhere, there are only so many of them and over sixty thousand acres of prairie and mountains to manage. These may not look like mountains to someone like you, coming out of the Rockies, but this is the most rugged section of country I've ever seen. Give it time. It will humble you."

"For the future of this preserve, let's hope not."

CHAPTER 8

October 1907

Fern and Noah saddled their horses for an early start. The dawn cast a dim array of colors across the high clouds. Hues of pink, shaded with the brightening tones of violet and blue, gave vivid portrayal of the awakening day. Fern spurred his mount to a rapid pace, with Noah keeping stride. Eager to make time, Fern led them to a pass between two rocky hills, navigating the scrub oaks and thick cedars. Momentary darkness remained under the forest canopy as they trekked through the dense undergrowth.

Small patches of grassy clearings led to sprawling meadows draped in morning dew. The trees became sparse as they rode out of the foliage. Noah followed Fern through a field. The horses' hooves clapped against the ground. Noah leaned to see solid rock underneath. His horse steadied its footing and slowed to a trot. The riders angled their mounts along a slope and bounded in several strides up the summit. The horses heaved for breath as Fern directed Noah to look westward.

"Watch," Fern said, then relaxed in the saddle. The sun breached the horizon, piercing the sky with warm rays. The intense beams illuminated the landscape before them. Noah watched the mountain shadow retreat from a brilliant spectacle of light. Piles of rocks, huge boulders, and jagged slopes appeared. The sunlight magnified the granite's auburn and red accents.

Fern addressed Noah. "What do you think?"

"I've never seen anything like this on the Great Plains."

"These are the Wichita Mountains," Fern said.

"They look like granite islands sticking up from a grassy ocean."

"Since when did you become sentimental? You sound like some writer publishing a journal."

Noah watched the range brighten in the rising sun. The years away from the southern plains subdued his memory. His acclimatization to the northern territories and the Rocky Mountains, with their cold climate and rugged elevation, suited his present life. But his return to the warmth and expanse of the Great Plains rejuvenated his soul with a sense of belonging. Ignoring Fern's prodding, he spoke from his heart.

"I've been to many places in the West. But none of them have the feeling that this place gives me." Noah looked across the valley to the adjacent mountain range. Fern saw the peace on Noah's face as he continued. "This feels like home."

"I've only seen you for one day, and already I am beginning to think age has humbled you. Can I dare say it? Has Noah Wrath learned to be happy?"

"Thanks for showing me this. It was well worth the trip down here. I didn't realize how much I've missed the southern plains."

"It's not only where you're from. It's who you are." Fern pulled the reins. "Well, the sun is up, and it's a beautiful day. Come on. We're just getting started."

Fern ventured farther into the mountains, leading Noah through a valley that separated the two ranges. Numerous rock formations, streams, and layered granite peaks detailed their journey. Fern described the various peaks and provided the names of the mountains he knew. The natural erosion of the mountains created rounded edges and flat surfaces in the coarse granite. The men departed the last of the trees and quickened their journey through the sage grass.

"Whoa!" Fern yelled. He stopped his horse and stared across the prairie.

"What do you see?" Noah asked.

Fern motioned ahead. A man held the reins to a horse, with a small girl standing next to him. "It's just a man and a little girl. Probably out for a ride."

Movement in the tall grass caught Noah's attention as he watched the distinct appearance of animal ears perking above the foliage. "Fern, look to the right of them. About fifty feet."

Fern searched the grass in time to see a large gray wolf rise above the grass. The predator stared at the man and girl before slowly moving in. "It's stalking them!" Fern reached for his revolver as four more wolves followed in pursuit. "It's a pack! They're attacking." He aimed his revolver at the lead wolf.

"Wait!" Noah pushed his arm down. "That man sees them."

"What is he doing? Is he waving at them?"

Noah watched the man in disbelief. "No. He's calling them."

"What?" Fern asked.

Both men watched as the wolves charged the man and girl. The small girl ran in front of the man and held up her arms. "I'm not going to allow this!" Fern yelled as he raised his revolver. Noah reached for Fern and forced his gloved hand over the hammer.

"They know the wolves!" Noah said.

The wolves got to within feet of the man and girl, then bounded around them. Fern gasped as the pack circled the two. Three wolves lunged at the man. He held out his hands and greeted the fearsome animals. They met him with gleeful barks. Two wolves played with the small girl, licking and whining while she stroked their fur.

Fern watched the spectacle. "What in the world is going on?"

"I think I know. Come on, but stay behind me. And holster that revolver before you scare them to death!"

"Scare them? I might have to check my drawers after watching that!" Fern replied as Noah took the lead.

They trotted toward the group. Noah deliberately pulled the reins, causing his horse to whinny. The man and girl noticed them. Noah watched as each wolf zeroed in on him with fearless aggression. The pack instinctively formed a wedge around the man and girl. The lead wolf moved forward, with the trailing wolves in pursuit.

"Okay, this could get interesting," Noah said as he stopped his mount.

Fern became nervous as the wolves spread out in formation. "All right, wise guy. Just so you know, if they get any closer, I'm shooting you first!"

Noah stared at the man and removed his cowboy hat. He waited to make eye contact and raised his right hand. Seconds passed as Noah could hear the lead wolf growl. His horse became uneasy at the daunting threat.

"Tseena!"

Both men looked ahead when the man made the sudden call. All at once, the wolves retreated and gathered behind the man and girl. They provided a final caress before the wolves ran away.

Fern sighed in relief. "Well, I learned two things this morning. The first is that I am never following you on horseback again. The second is that the man up there is Comanche."

"How do you know that?" Noah asked.

"*Tseena* is Comanche for 'wolf,'" Fern replied.

Noah became excited. "Let's go. I want to meet him."

"You don't listen very well, do you?" Fern said.

They dismounted several feet away. Walking their horses by the reins, they approached the man and girl and greeted them. The little girl, who appeared to be twelve years old, stepped forward. She smiled at Noah and Fern with unique confidence and introduced herself.

"My name is Mayuri. This is my grandfather, Kiyiya. And this is our horse, Firefly."

Noah knelt and removed his cowboy hat. "It's my pleasure, young lady. My name is Noah, and this is my friend, Fernando."

Mayuri waved at Fern as Noah approached Kiyiya and extended his hand. "Hello, sir." Kiyiya faced Noah. Both men became perplexed at the sight of each other. Noah searched his memory to remedy the strange recognition. "Somehow, you look familiar. Do I know you from somewhere?"

Fern stepped in front of Noah and extended his hand to Kiyiya. Then he said to Noah, "What's the matter with you? Can't you see he doesn't speak English?"

"Oh," Noah replied. He noticed his older age and seasoned posture.

Kiyiya motioned to Mayuri and whispered in her ear. She looked at Noah with eagerness. "My grandfather remembers you."

"What?" Fern asked. "Do you two know each other?"

Noah stepped closer to Kiyiya and looked into his eyes. A distraction in the forest behind him caught his attention as a wolf watched from the shadows. The sudden connection between Kiyiya and the wolf overwhelmed him. Noah inhaled deeply at the revelation from his memory. Then he exclaimed, "It's you!"

Kiyiya spoke a Comanche phrase to Mayuri. She addressed Noah and translated for her grandfather. "Fights for Wolves."

"What did you say?" Noah asked with urgency.

"Fights for Wolves. That is the name my grandfather gave you a long time ago," Mayuri replied.

"So that's what it means." He expressed his gratitude to Kiyiya. Kiyiya noticed his sincerity and gave noble acknowledgment.

Struck with another memory, Noah asked Kiyiya and Mayuri to wait, then rushed to his horse. He ripped open a saddlebag and ran his hand through the items. Overjoyed with his find, he hurried back to Kiyiya and held out his hand. Kiyiya saw an arrowhead on Noah's palm. He took the worn piece of flint. Observing it with remembrance, he placed it back on Noah's hand and spoke to Mayuri.

"He says it has been a long journey," she said.

"Yes. Please tell him it has been a very long journey. For both of us."

"What is going on?" Fern asked.

"Adobe Walls. We know each other from when the Comanche attacked Adobe Walls back in '74. When I went on that supply train. That's when we met."

"My grandfather remembers your gift," Mayuri said.

"Gift?" Noah asked.

"Saving his wolf," she replied.

"Yes, that time with the wolf and those gunmen."

"You fought to protect his wolf," Mayuri said.

Cherishing the splendor of the moment, Noah addressed Mayuri. "I am curious about what my friend and I saw earlier. What were those wolves doing with the two of you?"

Mayuri spoke to Kiyiya in Comanche and then replied to Noah. "They belong here. They are our wolves. We come to see them. They make my grandfather happy."

"I've never seen wolves like those before," Noah told her.

"They belong to these mountains. We know them."

"Yes, I understand," Noah said.

Kiyiya spoke to Mayuri, and she translated. "My grandfather wants to know where you are from."

"I am from Yellowstone. It is a national park in Wyoming. I work with animals at a sanctuary there."

"He wants to know which animals you work with."

"All kinds," Noah replied. "But mostly wolves."

Mayuri translated to Kiyiya and then spoke to Noah. "What are you doing here?"

"Some people asked me to come here. I am helping the preserve."

Mayuri translated. Kiyiya's eyes widened. Noah noticed a sudden avoidance in Kiyiya's demeanor toward him. Without hesitation, Kiyiya helped Mayuri onto the saddle and then mounted behind her.

Noah and Fern watched with confusion as Mayuri uttered an abrupt farewell. Avoiding further contact, Kiyiya spurred the horse and galloped away.

Fern and Noah continued their journey through the valley. The encounter with Kiyiya and Mayuri and their sudden departure weighed heavily on Noah's mind. He rode in silence, remembering the event with Kiyiya at Adobe Walls. The joy of finally understanding the name Kiyiya gave him long ago made him happy. The time since their first meeting humbled him as he recalled the passage of thirty-three years. Yearning for more conversation with the old Comanche, he shrugged off the disappointing end to their reunion and continued forward.

He and Fern navigated another forest and crossed a bridge leading to several small buildings.

"That's the preserve headquarters," Fern announced. They hitched their mounts and entered the main building. Three staff members stood next to a wall map, engaged in active discussion. Fern noticed the commotion and led Noah to the front desk. A woman sat with her back to the door, reading some documents.

"Who's in charge around here?" Fern asked and set his cowboy hat on the counter.

The woman gave a delighted grin. "It's about time you showed up! Did you need an invitation?" She embraced Fern. "It's great to see you again, Fern. What took you so long?"

"I was waiting on this guy to arrive." Fern acknowledged Noah. "Rebecca McGovern, meet Noah Wrath."

Noah removed his cowboy hat and said, "Ma'am."

"Hello," Rebecca said as she observed Noah with curiosity. "I've heard much about you, Mr. Wrath. You come with high regard."

"You can't believe everything Fern says, ma'am."

"I was referring to John Bruce," she replied.

"Oh. That's good to know." Noah put his hat back on and stepped away.

Rebecca watched Noah retreat.

"Give him time. He comes around to people eventually," Fern said.

"So much for the tough guy portrayal," Rebecca said. "I hope that is the only thing I've been told about him that is wrong."

"He may surprise you," Fern said.

"Not so far."

Fern hugged Rebecca again and grabbed his hat. He approached Noah, who was standing by the door, and said, "Try to get along with folks. Remember, you are here to help. They are not the enemy."

"You didn't tell me a woman was involved with this!"

"Must have slipped my mind." He slapped Noah on his shoulder. "I'll see you this evening."

"Where are you going?"

"Back to Cache. I have a ranch to run and a beautiful wife to see."

"And what exactly am I supposed to do?"

"You're coming with me, Mr. Wrath," Rebecca said as she walked between them.

Fern opened the door, and she walked outside. He struggled to contain his enjoyment of the situation as he said to Noah, "I believe you are going with her, Mr. Wrath. Allow me to hold the door for you."

Noah glared at Fern and reluctantly followed Rebecca, saying, "You haven't changed a bit."

They mounted their horses and rode farther across the preserve. Rebecca maintained a few horse lengths ahead of Noah. She kept her mount at a fast gallop. The terrain changed from scrub oaks and forests to contoured plains and open grasslands.

When they reached a fenced enclosure, Rebecca slowed her horse and stopped at the gate. Large posts with intricate wiring created a corral with open sheds to provide protection from the elements. Rebecca navigated her mount around the fencing, performing a final inspection of the construction.

"This is where the buffalo coming from the New York Zoological Park will be corralled." She admired the site. "Several people worked very hard to bring the buffalo back here. You should be proud, Mr. Wrath. You will be a part of history."

"I remember when they roamed in the millions," Noah said. "Now we are supposed to be proud for fifteen in a pen."

"Weren't you a buffalo hunter, Mr. Wrath?"

"What's that got to do with it?"

Rebecca raised her voice. "I can think of fifteen reasons!" She moved her horse forward and continued. "I never got to see buffalo in the millions. They were already gone. Killed by men like you. And now you want to mock the last chance we have to save them? Spare me your memories, Mr. Wrath. Because of buffalo hunters like you, all we have left is fifteen in a pen."

What had triggered his resentment became an odd sense of intrigue. Waiting several seconds to absorb the verbal attack from Rebecca, Noah spoke from his heart. "I can see you are very passionate about your work."

"Thanks to your past, there is nothing else to see here," Rebecca said. "Follow me. I have someone else for you to meet. Then you can go as you please."

"If they are anything like you, I most certainly will," Noah responded.

They continued riding along the foothills and slopes of the mountain range. Rebecca kept a steady distance from Noah. They reached a dry riverbed and prepared to cross. Driftwood and numerous round granite cobblestones of varying sizes littered the parched bottom. Rebecca steered her horse toward a sandy dune and jumped over a tree trunk.

A rattlesnake coiled on the other side and struck at the horse. The frightened mount stood on its hind legs and whinnied with fury. The sudden movement threw Rebecca onto the dune, and she landed hard on her back. Dazed from the impact, she wiped her nose, streaking blood across her sleeve. A few feet away, the distinct sound of rattling emanated from the recoiling diamondback.

Bam!

The granite sand burst into her eyes. Unable to see the rattlesnake, she kicked and screamed. Noah rushed to her side and carried her to the bank. He laid her in the soft grass and poured water from his canteen across her face. He pulled his knife from the sheath and removed his shirt. Cutting several strips from the fabric, he treated her bloody nose and wrapped the scrapes on her arms.

Rebecca regained her sight and looked into Noah's eyes as he held her. He wiped the last of the granite sand from her long, brunette hair. "That was close," Noah said.

Rebecca saw the rattlesnake, which was blown in half across the sand. Then she looked back at Noah, who was still holding her across his lap, and said, "Thank you."

"That was quite a fall. Are you hurt anywhere else?"

"I don't think so." The rush of the event subsided, leaving her shaken. "My head is pounding."

"Drink some more water. I'll see what I have in my saddlebags."

"Can you stay with me for a minute? I feel dizzy," Rebecca said.

Noah gently moved a strand of hair from her face and tucked it behind her ear. "Sure. Close your eyes if you need to." Rebecca looked at the snake again and moved closer to Noah. "Don't worry," he said. "It's dead."

"That was some . . . amazing . . . shot . . . you made," Rebecca stammered, then closed her eyes as Noah caressed her brow.

The wind blew softly through the dissipating heat. The steady breeze teased a strand of hair, tickling Rebecca's cheek as she opened her eyes. The approaching night cooled her as she rested under a large oak tree. She rubbed her aching head and focused to see Noah tending a fire. A spit was constructed above the shallow flames. She coughed and winced from the pain surging through her neck and back.

Noah knelt beside her with another canteen and asked, "How do you feel?"

"Like I've been thrown from a horse," Rebecca said. "How long was I out?"

Noah offered her water. "Most of the day. I figured you needed the rest."

"We need to get back to headquarters." Rebecca tried to get up and began to swoon.

"You are not ready to ride."

"I can handle myself, Mr. Wrath," Rebecca said. She reached for the ground to steady herself from the dizziness. "I just need a moment to—"

"No." Noah looked at her with defiance. "You need more rest. It is nearly dark, and you can't even sit up. We are staying put till morning." He untied her bedroll and spread a blanket over it. He positioned her saddlebag for a pillow and helped her move. Rebecca groaned from the pain and collapsed onto the soft bedding.

"When I start to feel better, we are leaving," she replied, out of breath.

"I said no."

"I am fully capable of taking care of myself. The staff are probably searching for us now," Rebecca said. "Why are you so conflicting about this?"

"Why are you so stubborn?" Noah yelled. His temper flared. "I've had enough of your belittling!"

Rebecca became alarmed at his anger and pulled the blanket close. Decades of living alone and on her terms strengthened her to rely on confidence and determination. She cowered to no one and accepted every obstacle as another challenge to be conquered. Knowing only sacrifice and turmoil with each day, she had proven herself throughout life. She demanded nothing short of success with every endeavor. She challenged any man or woman who dared to defy her resolve. Suddenly, the present situation made her feel helpless. Many attempted to intimidate her to overcome her. But with Noah, it was a level of dominance she had never experienced before. Uncomfortable with his overpowering presence, she reluctantly surrendered.

Noah saw her retreat and composed himself. "Forgive me. I should not have yelled at you." He searched for words to continue. "I usually know what to do in situations like this, but since you're a, well . . ."

"A woman?" Rebecca asked. Noah nodded without looking at her. She hid her smile. "Are there not many women back at Yellowstone?"

"Ma'am, there aren't many women in all of Wyoming."

Rebecca snickered. "I see." She noticed his subtle reservation and realized he was simply trying to be considerate. Tired and weary from the day, she decided to lower her guard and offer empathy. "Maybe we got off on the wrong foot, Mr. Wrath. If it is okay with you, and since we must work together, would you care to start over?"

Noah knelt beside her. His blue eyes glistened in the firelight as she saw his chiseled face and broad shoulders. He removed his cowboy hat and leaned closer. "Do you like wild turkey?"

"What?"

Noah pointed at the spit. Two large, plucked birds hung on the crossbar, simmering to a golden brown. "I shot them earlier when I went looking for your horse." He faced Rebecca with an inviting grin. "Hungry?"

Rebecca released an invigorated reply: "Starving."

They finished supper and relaxed near the fire. The night sky was filled with flickering stars. The mountains awakened with the inhabitants of darkness as various noises of the night echoed throughout the valley. Coyotes howled as Noah placed more logs on the fire. The flames reached upward with brilliant light for added protection against wandering predators. Rebecca curled the blanket around her body. The sound of numerous cicadas chirped from the limbs above.

They talked about various topics. Noah inquired about the preserve and asked several questions about his role. Rebecca eagerly engaged and asked about his experiences. They shared stories that dwindled the night with renewed conversation.

"What do you think about predator drives? Would that help get them off the preserve?" Rebecca asked.

"It would be difficult in this terrain. From what I have seen so far, there are too many places to hide. And we would need ten times the staff to cover even a small part of the preserve. Then the question becomes what to do with them once they are driven off the preserve."

"Poachers are everywhere," Rebecca added. "The illegal hunting is rampant. We have certainly had our share of challenges. I think the problem is they want all predators, mostly the wolves, off the preserve before the buffalo arrive from New York."

"That will be difficult to do. Are there a lot of wolves here?" Noah asked.

"It depends on who you ask. We don't have an exact number. What do you do at Yellowstone to capture them?"

"We use trap cages. But Yellowstone has a lot of territory. We don't have enough cages, and we can't capture them all," Noah replied. "Even if we did, we would need more staff to cover a fraction of the park."

Rebecca watched the coals burn bright orange. She looked at Noah, who was also observing the fire, and altered the topic. "I hear you have a gift with wolves."

Noah kept his eyes on the fire. "Mr. Bruce has a big mouth."

"You're not denying it?"

"I'd rather not entertain it," Noah said.

"Why?"

"If you are asking genuinely, it is something that is easier seen than said."

"Fair enough," Rebecca said. "And yes, I was asking genuinely."

His better judgment was against it, but Rebecca lured him in. "It's a feeling, mostly. Like when you recognize someone you have not seen for a long time. You can't remember their name or where you last saw them, but you know them."

"How do you know it won't attack you?"

"I can tell once we make eye contact. It becomes very calming, as though a bond has been formed. There becomes a trust between us," Noah said.

"Nothing of what you said is befitting of your last name. Is that your family name?" Rebecca asked.

"You can blame Fern for that."

"How so?" Rebecca asked.

"He pretty much saved me. Or he saved me from myself."

Rebecca waited. Seconds passed without word from Noah before she asked, "And?"

"It's a rather long story."

"Consider it restitution for keeping me here all night," Rebecca said with a grin. "You may continue."

Noah noticed her brown eyes concentrated on him. Her long hair cascaded along each cheek. The warm glow from the fire accentuated her facial features and magnified her natural beauty. Their eyes met for a moment as Noah quickly looked away. A strange insecurity invaded his impenetrable confidence. He willingly shared personal discussion with Fern without reservation, but never with someone he did not know. And never with a woman. He took a deep breath and wandered into vulnerability.

"Fern found me on the plains a long time ago. I was in my teens. He took me in, and we became friends. I didn't talk very much at the start, so he gave me my last name. I looked up to him. He offered me a job hunting buffalo, and I've known him ever since."

"Why did he name you Wrath?" Rebecca asked.

Noah hesitated. "You know, there are some questions you shouldn't ask, Ms. McGovern. This is one of those questions."

"And you called *me* stubborn?" She raised her eyebrows.

"I'm surprised Fern and Mr. Bruce haven't told you everything about me," Noah said.

"At the moment, I'm not asking them."

"Ma'am, you are a feisty one. I'll give you that." Rebecca waited sternly as Noah continued with another deep breath. "I was working a cattle drive down in south Texas. We got rustled. Many people were killed. One other and I held out until he got shot trying to protect me. Once night fell, the rustlers took the herd. I tracked them to a ravine several miles away. There were eight of them."

"Sounds like you were outnumbered," Rebecca said. "What did you do?"

"I wasn't sure what I wanted to do. So, I waited until they were asleep. I did to them what they did to me."

"What?" Rebecca asked. She noticed Noah become tense.

He stared at the flames and answered without remorse. "I killed them one by one."

"Oh." Rebecca hid her shock. "Who was it that tried to protect you?"

"My father. The cowhands were my brothers. I lost my mother and sister too." Noah squinted from resurrected memory. "Fern heard what I had done and was afraid that either the law or other rustlers would come looking for me. So he changed my name."

Rebecca waited to reply, careful to choose her words. "I guess I was wrong. Your name is quite befitting. I am sorry about your family. That is horrible."

"That was a long time ago, Ms. McGovern. And it's got nothing to do with a name. I've struggled with myself every day over what happened to my family and what I did to those men. All I knew was killing. Accuracy and speed with a revolver and knives came natural to me. I used those abilities on men and buffalo. It didn't matter. Fern gave me that name because of my anger. The more I killed, the less I felt. But the pain never went away." Rebecca remained silent as Noah faced her and said, "I vowed never to kill in anger again so that maybe God would forgive me."

"God looks at your heart," Rebecca said. "What does your heart say?"

Noah answered without hesitation. "I can't forgive myself."

Rebecca inched closer. She watched the heat rise from the fire and disappear into the starry night sky. Focusing on the brightest star, she prepared her mind and resurrected her evaded past.

"When I met my late husband, Andrew, we were both eager to make a difference. We wanted to save the buffalo and build great animal sanctuaries across the country. He used to say that life without a purpose to serve is selfish. He was going to run for office and be the voice for those who didn't have one. He wanted to be the voice for wildlife. One day, he went to your Yellowstone, right as it was being established. He couldn't wait to see the results of the work he and others had done to create the first national park. All he wanted to do was have a place to protect the buffalo and all wildlife. He walked up on a buffalo herd feeding near a river. Some poachers were already there. He tried to stop them from shooting the buffalo. Then they killed him for it."

Rebecca lowered her head and cleared her throat. She wiped her eyes and stared into the flames. "I've struggled with myself every day over what happened to my husband. I wanted him to go. It gave him a purpose. And he died for it." She looked at Noah with sadness. "Forgiveness is all we have so that we *can* live."

"I am very sorry, ma'am, if my coming from Yellowstone caused you any unintended anguish. You have suffered a long time."

She observed him as though she was peering into his soul. "What really brought you to Oklahoma? Is your friend Fern the only reason?"

"I guess I would say I want to help the preserve. And the money was hard to turn down too."

"Of course," Rebecca added. "Like I said, we have to live."

Her words resonated within him. A genuine feeling overcame him as he gave a sincere reply. "I don't blame you for getting mad at me about being a buffalo hunter. I can't change my past. But I sure want to change who I am. All I've done is survive life. I'm tired of that. I want to live life. Like you do."

"Now you're talking from your heart." Rebecca felt her intrigue for Noah deepen. "I'm sorry for being stubborn, Mr. Wrath. I want to say it is an occupational hazard. But, just like your abilities with guns and knives, the more I avoid, the less I feel."

Noah leaned closer to see her eyes. Their expressions merged with arousing interest as he responded with yearning appeal. "I've spent my life on my own. I stayed away from people and lived in anger because I had no one to talk to. No one who really understands like you do." He removed his cowboy hat and embraced vulnerability. "And please, call me Noah."

She blinked softly with welcomed acceptance, "And I'm Rebecca." Their eyes joined with visual enticement, allowing the moment to pass without words. Attraction sparked in their gaze as Rebecca felt her heart flutter. Noah saw her with warm regard as she watched the rising flames. "I'm beginning to think your gift of feelings is not limited to wolves."

CHAPTER 9

October 1907

Morning arrived with a chorus of black-capped vireos chirping their joy from the neighboring trees. Their harmonious tones welcomed the coming day as Noah and Rebecca prepared for an early start. They packed their belongings and readied their mounts. The absence of breakfast motivated their departure as Noah helped Rebecca to her saddle. She moved through the lingering soreness while Noah fastened the stirrups to her boots. Reluctant to engage with her horse for fear of added pain, she surrendered to hope and prepared to ride.

"I'll ride lead this time," Noah said. "We don't need you finding more critters the hard way. Your poor horse has suffered enough."

"I assume that is your attempt at humor? Just so you know, if you get thrown, I'm not stopping."

"Sounds like you got some rest."

"Sleeping on the ground has its limits, but I'm better today."

"I'm glad you agreed to stay the night," Noah said.

"I'll give you that one, but only that one."

They led their mounts across the prairie. Rebecca directed him to a rocky draw along one of the mountain slopes. Three horses waited with their reins tied to trees. Noah and Rebecca dismounted as she yelled into the canyon. A reply echoed across the granite walls.

Finding Refuge

They hiked over the rugged terrain, navigating between boulders and rock formations. Finally, a staff member called to them and waved.

Noah and Rebecca reached the staff and she introduced everyone. "Noah, this is Trey Doyle. He has overseen the setting of our wolf traps in the field. The senior members hired him to direct that part of the plan."

"Mr. Wrath, it's a pleasure," Trey said. "We heard you two were missing. Glad to see that isn't the case." Noah thanked him as Rebecca avoided further discussion of their disappearance. "I hear you oversee the Yellowstone project. I'll bet that is quite a feat to manage. Do you have a lot of wolves up there?"

"Enough to keep us busy. This is a sizeable project you have here," Noah said. "I was wondering if you have a breed of wolf indigenous to this area."

"Not to my knowledge. At least none that I have seen. Mostly the gray wolf species and a lot of coyotes. Why? Have you seen anything?" Trey asked.

Noah shook his head, recalling the unique wolves he saw with Kiyiya and Mayuri. Reluctant to continue, he changed the topic. "How many gray wolves have you saved?"

"I don't know. Not as many as we would hope for. It makes me wonder if we are too late for larger numbers. The poaching around here is guaranteed if the wolves venture outside the preserve."

"You have a lot of traps in place. I saw your map on the headquarters wall. Are you trapped out?" Noah asked.

"We keep a close eye on the traps and get whatever we catch to the holding pens as soon as possible."

"What do you do with them then?" Noah asked.

"We have a ranch in Texas we ship them to. It's a holding area for the wolves until the senior members make further arrangements. It's the only choice we have at the moment. There isn't much calling for gray wolves. And with the Wichitas being the only mountain range in this part of the territory, there is nowhere else for them to go," Trey replied. "I use my pair of German shepherds to help sniff them out and round them up. We corral the wolves we can before they wander off the preserve."

Noah stared at Trey without response. He reviewed their cage traps and provided advice and answers to questions. Rebecca thanked the staff members for their work and walked to her horse with Noah. They rode to the headquarters building and checked in. The team there welcomed their arrival and provided ample first aid, nourishment, and beverages. Noah and Rebecca recovered from their adventurous evening and parted to tidy for the day.

Refreshed from an hour in his quarters, Noah walked the headquarters grounds and met more staff members. He entered the main building and noticed Rebecca resting in a chair.

"Are you feeling better?" he asked.

"Nothing a hot bath can't remedy. How do you like your quarters?"

"When compared to a log cabin with a dirt floor, it has appeal," Noah said. He looked around the room for other staff and addressed Rebecca in a low voice. "Did you think it was odd that Mr. Doyle did not know how many gray wolves have been saved?"

"Maybe he didn't know at the time."

"It's his job to know," Noah said. "How can he be in charge of the trap cages and have no idea how many wolves he has caught? And I'm not sure I understand using German shepherds to herd wolves. They aren't cattle. How long did you say he has worked here?"

"Easy, Noah. You don't even know him yet."

"Do you?"

A staff member hurried through the front door, calling, "Rebecca! I've been looking all over for you. There is a little girl who has been waiting outside since early this morning, asking to see the man from Yellowstone." She looked at Noah. "Is that you?"

Noah approached the door, with Rebecca following closely behind. He opened it to see Mayuri sitting on the bottom step. He sat next to her as Rebecca knelt in front of them. Mayuri had an opened journal spread across her lap. She focused on her writing, eager to finish before any interruption. Noah and Rebecca watched her childish determination as she completed a short sentence and closed her book.

"Hi there," Rebecca said. "What are you writing?"

"A poem. I write poetry for my grandfather. He likes it. We try to make songs out of them, but I'm not very good at that yet," Mayuri replied.

"Are you the little girl I met earlier?" Noah asked. "Is your name Mayuri?"

"Yes."

"How did you get here?" Rebecca asked.

"My grandfather brought me on his horse. It was too far to walk. I didn't mind walking. I like walking. I sing with the birds. But my grandfather didn't want me to get tired."

"Or lost?" Rebecca added.

"I don't get lost. I know my way around the mountains. My mom and dad and I live across the road from my grandfather. He watches me during the day. We come to the mountains all the time."

Rebecca was impressed with her confident demeanor. "What can we do for you, Mayuri? You have come a long way."

The girl addressed Noah. "My grandfather wants to meet you. His name is Kiyiya, in case you forgot already."

"No, I remember both of you. And I would like that very much. When would he like to meet? Would tomorrow be good for him?"

"He wants to meet you now."

Noah responded without challenge. "Okay. I guess my day became available. Do you mind if I invite my friend Rebecca to come with us?" he asked.

"Yes. She seems nice. I like her. She can come too," Mayuri replied.

"All right then. Let's get our horses and go see your grandfather," Noah said.

They prepared their mounts, with Mayuri joining Rebecca, then rode toward Cache. Mayuri gave detailed directions as they ventured through the mountains, taking trails Rebecca had not seen before. Impressed with the girl's navigation skills, they followed a road leading to a small ranch house with a barn and fenced pasture. An old man sat in a rocking chair on the wraparound front porch.

They approached the house and dismounted by the steps. The man stood from his chair and embraced Mayuri with a loving hug. He held her hand and walked to Noah and Rebecca. Mayuri kept her journal close and interpreted for him as he spoke in Comanche.

"This is my grandfather, Kiyiya. He thanks you for coming." Mayuri whispered, "He speaks English when he wants to. I teach him new words after school. He likes it when I speak Comanche." She resumed her normal volume. "He wants you to sit with him."

Kiyiya offered them a seat.

Noah was eager to see him again. "Mayuri," he said. "Will you ask Kiyiya why you both left so suddenly when we met yesterday?"

She interpreted for Kiyiya, and they spoke for several minutes. Noah and Rebecca listened to their Comanche language, intrigued by their dialect. Mayuri became irritated with some words and reasoned with Kiyiya for explanation. They provoked each other and provided hand gestures to emphasize their meaning. Content with their conversation, Mayuri thought of a reply.

"Do you come to harm the wolves like the others do?" she asked Noah.

Noah was puzzled by the unexpected question. "No. I am here to help them. We want to make sure they do not harm the buffalo when they arrive."

Mayuri spoke to Kiyiya and then to Noah. "The Comanche are proud that the buffalo are returning. But my grandfather is concerned about what will happen to the wolves. They are being taken away or killed."

"We are trying to stop that," Noah said.

"You can't," Mayuri replied. "They have taken too many wolves already."

"Who is taking the wolves?" Rebecca asked. "Have you seen someone?"

"The buffalo hunter in the mountains. He is on the preserve. We have seen him and the other men take the wolves. Sometimes they kill them."

Rebecca said, "Honey, there are no buffalo hunters on the preserve anymore. Can you be more specific?"

Mayuri spoke to Kiyiya. He became silent. He allowed the moment to pass and stated a brief sentence, which Mayuri then explained.

"My grandfather is angry that the wolves are nearly gone. He wants to know why the buffalo can live here but the wolves cannot. It was not the wolves that made the buffalo disappear."

Noah sighed with remorse. He felt the burden of Kiyiya's words weigh heavily upon him. The regret of his past as a buffalo hunter came back to haunt him. He looked at Kiyiya with a humble appearance, unable to respond. He noticed Rebecca watching him out of the corner of his eye.

"What do I say to that?" Noah asked.

Kiyiya observed Noah's grief and spoke to Mayuri. "He wants to know more about your gift."

"Gift?" Noah asked.

Kiyiya asked, "How do you know the wolves?"

Noah watched Kiyiya with curious suspicion. Excitement swelled within him as he responded. "It is a feeling I have with them. A connection."

Mayuri interpreted. Kiyiya understood. He began speaking in small sentences to allow Mayuri time to translate.

"My grandfather says the wolves are gone. He thinks you call them the gray wolves. He thinks they have either been taken or killed like the buffalo in his day. But you must help us. He says you must save the Wichita wolves. There is only one pack left that we know of. They are special wolves. They live only in these mountains."

"Wichita wolves?" Noah asked Rebecca. She shrugged in confusion.

"I can show you. We have some in our barn. We are taking care of them," Mayuri said. She faced Rebecca. "Your friends at the preserve said you are an animal biologist."

"Yes, that's right," Rebecca said.

"Are you a doctor for animals?"

"Not exactly. I study them."

Mayuri seemed confused. She grabbed her journal. "Maybe you can help them anyway. Come with us. We will show you our Wichita wolves."

Mayuri and Kiyiya led them to the back of their barn, where there was a boarded stall. Mayuri entered the gate and stepped through piles of yellow straw. Kiyiya stood at the opening while Noah and Rebecca peered over the wall. Mayuri held a small animal in front of Rebecca.

"That's a wolf pup," Rebecca said. "It looks like a newborn. How long have you had it?"

Mayuri pointed to the corner as Kiyiya removed a mound of straw, revealing a female wolf nursing three more pups. "She gave birth last week," the girl said. "We brought her here from the mountains."

"Oh my," Rebecca said as she hurried around the wall. She knelt beside the mother to see the hungry pups. The mother remained still. She raised her head with a feeble attempt to growl at Rebecca. "This wolf is sick."

"Can you help her? There is something wrong with her leg," Mayuri said as she looked at the injury. "She can't walk."

Rebecca triaged the leg. "It could be a break, and it looks infected. Where did you find this wolf?"

Mayuri glanced at Kiyiya and then back to Rebecca. "In the mountains."

"Where in the mountains?" Noah asked. "How did you catch her?" He held the pup and scratched behind its ears. It calmed and sniffed Noah. He knelt next to the mother and leaned forward to make eye contact. The injured wolf pawed at him and wrestled against Rebecca to reach Noah. Favoring her injured leg, she whined and sat next to him.

Kiyiya watched the wolf befriend Noah. He spoke to Mayuri.

"These are my grandfather's wolves," the little girl said. "The male wolf was captured. We went looking for him to save him, but he was already gone."

Noah watched Mayuri avoid him as he spoke to Kiyiya. "Mayuri, you and Kiyiya took this wolf from a cage trap, didn't you?"

Mayuri did not answer him as Kiyiya surprised him with a response. "Yes."

"Noah, look at this," Rebecca said. "The features of this wolf are different from the gray wolf. For an adult female, she is not as large, but the fur and the size of her head contrast with that of a gray wolf. And she is not a coyote." She became excited. "I'm not certain, because they are rare, but I think this might be a red wolf."

"Are red wolves special?" Noah asked.

"Yes. And native to these mountains." She addressed Mayuri with eagerness. "I have medicine at the headquarters for the infection. We can wrap her leg and help it heal. How are you keeping them fed?"

Mayuri showed her scraps and leftovers from their meals.

Kiyiya summoned Mayuri to his side. They spoke briefly before Mayuri translated for Noah and Rebecca. "My grandfather is happy you are helping the wolves. He wants to know if you can find the others and save them from the bad men."

Noah became concerned. "This could get interesting," he said.

"It already has," Rebecca said as she winked. "We will do our best. But we will need your help to find them."

Mayuri cheered and told Kiyiya. He nodded his appreciation and spoke to Mayuri. She became puzzled and addressed Noah. "My grandfather is grateful to both of you. The wolves mean so much to him." She sorted her thoughts. "He wants to know if you have the arrowhead with you."

Noah reached into his pocket and showed it to her. "I thought this might come in handy today with your invitation," he said.

Kiyiya urged Noah to extend his hand with the arrowhead. He placed a small wooden cross over the arrowhead and spoke in Comanche.

"He says your name is no longer Fights for Wolves," Mayuri said.

Kiyiya wrote on one of Mayuri's journal pages and tore it from the binder. Then he handed it to Noah and spoke to Mayuri. She faced Noah with enthusiasm. "Your name is Knows the Wolf. And he wrote a Bible verse on the paper for you. He wants you to read it out loud."

Noah took the paper and read the verse. "I am sending you out as sheep in the midst of wolves, so be wise as serpents and innocent as doves." Noah faced Kiyiya. "I know this verse. It's from Matthew. Thank you."

He lifted the cross from his hand and spoke in English. "Make this your strength." He removed the arrowhead from his palm and said, "Not this." He directed Noah to place the arrowhead back in his pocket. "What was." He placed the cross back on Noah's hand. "What is."

Tears streamed down Noah's face. The burden of anger, carried for decades, lifted from his soul. A feeling of release swept over him. A calmness he'd never before allowed himself to experience soothed his distraught mind.

"My grandfather likes you. He said your gift is also your purpose," Mayuri said. "It is what you must do."

Noah wiped his eyes. "What purpose is that?"

"That's all he said," Mayuri replied.

Noah chuckled. "Yep, this is going to get interesting."

They gathered around the wolf and pups while Rebecca checked each one. They quietly had concern for their survival but became more reassured with Rebecca's tending care. Using materials found in the barn, she fashioned a splint for the broken leg and cleaned the injury. Noah admired her experience with the wolves. As he watched her skill with each animal, he began to admire her for more than her professional title. His reluctance to work with Rebecca continued to subside. Her confidence impressed him because of the strength she possessed in a firm stature but gentle character. With each passing moment, his curious interest in her became a subtle attraction.

Mayuri finished another conversation with Kiyiya in Comanche, then addressed Noah and Rebecca. "We will take you to the den tomorrow to save the other wolves. There are four of them. Two males and two females. My grandfather thinks one of the females is pregnant."

Kiyiya drew a map describing the location. Rebecca became excited. "That looks familiar," she said. "I remember that area from previous surveys." She helped Kiyiya add landmarks and terrain features. They refined the map together and shared mutual enthusiasm.

"This is great! I must tell the staff so they can help protect that area," Rebecca said. "Tell your grandfather we will do all we can for the remaining wolves at the den." She spoke to Noah. "We need to save this breed."

"What we need is a plan," Noah told her.

"We need some help too."

"I'd prefer we keep this between us. The fewer people who know about this, the better. If these wolves are as special as you say they are, we do not need a lot of attention," Noah said.

"Trey Doyle is in charge of the wolf project. I'll let him know in case he has some cage traps in that area we can use. I'm going to headquarters to get things ready for tomorrow," Rebecca said. "Are you coming?"

"I'll catch up. I'm going to pay Fern a visit. We can use his help," Noah replied. "I'll meet you at headquarters later tonight."

Mayuri translated for Kiyiya with a frown. Then she said, "My grandfather says he will meet you at the headquarters building in the morning. But I have to stay with my parents." She pouted as she played with the wolf pups.

Noah looked at the cross still in his hand. "Looks like this just became a rescue mission."

Rebecca looked at the cross, nudged Noah as she walked by, and asked, "For the wolves or for you?"

CHAPTER 10

October 1907

Rebecca packed her saddlebag and hurried through breakfast. The amber glow of the early dawn pierced the night sky. She studied the Wichita National Forest and Game Preserve map again, confident of the location and terrain features. She loaded a revolver and secured it in the holster. A final check of her supplies and food was all that remained. She piled everything on her desk and finished the last of her coffee. She looked at the clock and panicked at her lateness. Darkness still prevailed as she grabbed her coat and ran out of the headquarters building.

She approached the stables and searched for her mount. Then she heard someone cry, "Rebecca!"

She noticed a staff member running toward her, holding a lantern. The staff member waved a piece of paper while yelling for her to stop.

"I didn't know you were leaving so early," the woman said. "This arrived late yesterday evening from Cache. I couldn't find you. The sender demanded that it be given to you in person." She handed Rebecca a telegram.

"Can I use your lantern?" Rebecca asked. The staff member held the light over the paper as Rebecca read to herself: *Senior members have no plan. Possible contingencies. Save all wolves you can. Tell*

Fern and Noah. Arriving tomorrow. John Bruce. She lowered the telegram. "When did you say you received this?"

"Late yesterday. I hope I'm not too late."

"That means he arrives today," Rebecca mumbled to herself. Her mind raced with skepticism as she addressed the staff member. "No, you are fine. Thank you for getting this to me." Rebecca saddled her horse and stowed her gear. She shoved the telegram in her coat pocket and urged her mount quickly to the west range.

She bounded across the terrain, staying in the safety of the open prairie. The valley began to awaken with sparse light to guide her direction. She rode through the high sage grass and approached the designated terrain feature—a large, angled hill of rock that rose sharply from the ground. Its distinct feature served as the marker for the road leading from the preserve to the small town of Cache. Rebecca stood in her stirrups to see several riders waiting with a wagon at the base of the rock formation.

She approached to be greeted by Noah, Fern, Cecilia, and Kiyiya. They dismounted and gathered under a tree. Fern spread a preserve map across a granite rock and began pinpointing the location of the wolf den with Kiyiya. Identifying the suspected area, they determined their route and began to mount.

"Wait," Rebecca said. "I received a telegram from John Bruce." She read the telegram and addressed the group. "His message is odd. It doesn't sound like him. He wouldn't send this unless something was wrong."

Fern took the telegram and read it again. "Possible contingencies?"

"That confused me too," Rebecca said. "He wrote this as if to hide what he is really wanting to say."

"But can't," Fern said.

"What do you think he means?" Rebecca asked.

"Something else could be involved with removing the wolves from the preserve," Fern replied.

"Or someone," Noah added.

"True," Fern said. "And if the senior members have no plan but still want the wolves off the preserve before the buffalo arrive . . ."

"By any means possible?" Noah asked and stared at Fern.

"We need to get moving. If John is arriving today, we need to have something to tell him," Fern said.

"All right. Kiyiya says the wolf den is over that rise. We will locate the den, set the cage traps, and work in shifts to check them," Noah said. "Cecilia will stay with the wagon. That is rough ground, from the looks of it, and the wagon won't make it. Let's go."

The terrain challenged their effort, forcing them to change their route several times. Granite boulders, dense foliage, and narrow ravines covered the rise. They dismounted and continued the trek on foot.

Kiyiya led the group through the winding terrain features. His steady pace impressed the followers as they heaved breaths to keep up. They traversed a granite outcropping as Kiyiya paused. He looked ahead while the group peered around the rock formation.

A small enclosure, embedded in the granite, was camouflaged behind a cedar. They watched the den for several minutes, listening for any sounds. Kiyiya approached the den. He stopped in front of the opening. The rest of the group encircled the den.

"Wolves are gone," Kiyiya said and pointed at the ground.

"What do you mean?" Rebecca asked.

Fern studied the disturbed earth. "This looks like part of a boot print. I can see the heel. Whoever did this tried to cover their tracks."

"They brushed their tracks," Noah said. He emerged from the foliage with a broken cedar branch. "I've seen this tactic before. Poachers use cedar branches to brush the dirt and erase their tracks. Whoever tried this must have been in a hurry. All they did was make it more obvious that they were here."

"Come," Kiyiya said. He directed them to see some embedded lines in the ground.

"Those are cage trap markings. Look, you can see where the weight of the metal bottom sank in the earth," Fern said. "Someone beat us to it."

"Or they knew we were coming," Noah said. He walked in front of Rebecca. "This is not a coincidence. Someone knew about this den and that we were coming. Who else at headquarters was aware of what we were doing here today?"

"No one!" Rebecca yelled. "What are you saying? These have to be poachers."

"If they are, they are well-informed poachers. Who else knew about this?"

Rebecca was in disbelief. She searched her mind for reason and attempted to remember any details. "When we spoke with Kiyiya at his home and discovered the special breed, the Wichita wolves, I went back to headquarters and . . ." She froze in sudden realization. "Oh no."

"Come," Kiyiya said, looking away from the den.

"Wait a moment," Noah responded, then continued talking to Rebecca. "Who did you tell?"

"I filed a report to John Bruce. But I didn't send it. I had the staff send it."

"Who sent it?" Noah asked again.

"Trey Doyle. But he wouldn't—"

"Was he hired by John?" Noah asked.

Rebecca became pale with distress. "No. He was hired by the senior members."

"Come now!" Kiyiya shouted. They rushed to him and saw Kiyiya pointing below. "Wagon tracks."

"This was a coordinated effort," Fern said. "Those tracks are leading away from the preserve. Whoever did this knew what they were doing and had the resources to pull it off." He looked at Noah and Rebecca. "Someone has sold you out."

Noah closed his eyes. He took a deep breath and noticed that Rebecca was distraught with grief. He searched his memory for a remedy for the situation. A recollection of his past profession invaded his mind. A confidence known only in the wilds of his earlier days became evident as the source of his answer to the dilemma before him. Thinking of his prior traits, he approached Kiyiya with a hunter's resolve.

Noah looked at the wagon tracks below and said, "We need to find them." He addressed Rebecca, "Kiyiya, Fern, and I will track the poachers. I want you to go back with Cecilia."

"No. I'm going with all of you."

"No, you're not. This isn't some fence-building project for buffalo. Until we know who we are dealing with, you need to let us handle this."

"What makes you think it would be any different if you were not here?" Rebecca asked. "This is my job, Noah. It is my responsibility as much as it is yours. I'm going."

Kiyiya watched their argument unfold and walked between them. He took Rebecca's hand. "If bad men knew my wolves were here, they may know where the others are too. Please check that Mayuri and the wolf pups are safe."

Rebecca felt disappointment and acknowledged Kiyiya. He thanked her and started down the hill. She frowned at Noah, "He has a point. Trey knows I came from Kiyiya's home when I filed the report. He knows there are special-breed wolf pups there. I'll go check on Mayuri. But I want you to know that I am doing this for her, not you." She brushed by his side to leave.

Noah grabbed her arm. "What is the matter with you? Why do you insist on being so stubborn? Can't you see I want you to be safe?" He struggled to find his next words. "I don't know what is going to happen or who these people are. But I do know that I could not live with myself if something bad happened to you." He thought before continuing. "If the men who took these wolves know about the wolf pups at Kiyiya's barn, you need to have a plan. You can't expect them to . . ." He looked into her eyes with a sudden loss for words. Stammering, he stepped aside and marched down the hill.

Rebecca watched him leave as Fern approached her from the other side of the wolf den. "He's right," Fern said. "Think it through in case things get tricky with those pups. Talk to Cecilia. She can help." Rebecca kept her attention upon Noah. Fern saw her discontent. "Listen, I've known Noah a long time. He is a loner. He can't stand to be around people very long. It's not that he doesn't like them. He doesn't like himself. And because of that, he hardly ever talks to anyone about anything. It's his way of coping with his past, I guess."

"You were late getting to us this morning," he said. "All he talked about the whole time we were waiting was riding to the headquarters and making sure you were okay." He winked at her and started his way down the slope. "He's never wanted to do that for anyone else before."

The wind blew through the prairie grasses with a gentle sway as Noah, Fern, and Kiyiya peered over a rise. The open terrain spread toward the horizon, with the Wichita Mountains providing the skyline behind them. The Great Plains made its dominant presence known between the scattered granite peaks of the westward mountain range. The three men remained prone in the grass, watching a lone wagon with three mounted escorts navigate the landscape.

Fern spied on the unsuspecting group through binoculars. "I only see a driver with the wagon. I can't tell how many wolves there are. They boarded the sides of the crate. For terrain as rugged as this, they are in a hurry to get somewhere. I'm surprised we caught up to them before dark."

"They're headed southwest," Noah said. "Where are they going way out here?"

"I don't know. A holding pen, maybe?" Fern handed the binoculars to Kiyiya.

Noah checked his revolver. "It's time to find out."

"Now, wait a minute, gunslinger. We are outnumbered. And I don't think Kiyiya signed up for a shootout," Fern said. "Neither did I."

"Who said anything about a shootout?" Noah looked at Kiyiya. "What do you think we should do?"

He lowered the binoculars and looked at the setting sun. "Wait for darkness."

"And then what?" Noah asked.

"We get my wolves."

"What about those poachers? They are armed."

Kiyiya saw an escort far in front of the wagon. The escort, who was scouting for a safe route, led the group forward through the developing night. "You were a buffalo hunter?" he asked.

"Yes. A long time ago. Why?"

Kiyiya maintained a calmness to his voice that portrayed patience. Noah listened intently for what the wise man would say. The rare time he'd spent with the Comanche had provided an experience Noah cherished. He felt a connection to Kiyiya, both from their past at Adobe Walls and through their shared gift for wolves. Noah knew he was living a special moment. With each passing hour, his time with Kiyiya brought admiration and peace to his life.

Kiyiya came to a knee and looked at the wagon team with a noble guise. His presence seemed to complement the pristine surroundings of the plains. Observing Kiyiya in the dusk, he saw the presence of living history. In every way, Kiyiya exuded a sense of tradition and greatness to the plains that transcended time.

He looked down at Noah, who was still prone in the grass. "How did you stop a small herd when you hunted buffalo?"

Noah became confused. "Do you mean a stampede?" Kiyiya stared at him without reply. Unsure of the man's meaning, Noah proceeded. "I would sight the lead buffalo and . . ." His eyes widened with revelation. He rolled to his side and praised Kiyiya. "You, sir, are a genius."

"What are you two talking about? Do we have a plan or not?" Fern asked.

Noah resonated with pride. "Yes. We have a plan. We are going hunting."

"What?" Fern asked.

"Come on. We will need your horse for this."

The wagon rolled slowly over the rugged prairie. The driver stood precariously next to the seat, watching the terrain for obstacles. He slowed the team as the last of the evening light faded. The leading escort yelled at the driver, urging him to increase speed. The remaining two escorts guided the team on either side of the wagon. One wagon wheel sank in a prairie dog burrow, causing the rig to sway. Upset, the driver shouted at the lead escort and angled the team away from the hole.

"Hurry it up! We were supposed to be there before dark!" an escort bellowed at the driver.

"A fine job you're doing! I've hit every critter den and rock since we left the mountains. Find a better route. I can't see anything in the dark anyway," the driver responded.

"What's that up ahead?" an escort asked.

The men peered through the darkness to see the silhouette of a bareback horse grazing in the grass. It blocked their path forward as the lead escort continued.

"Looks like it has wandered off!" he yelled back to the wagon.

"Take it! We can tie it to the back of the wagon," the driver ordered. "Did you hear me?" He stopped the wagon team and waited several seconds without a reply. Unable to see farther ahead, he signaled to another escort. "Ride up there and see if he needs any help."

The escort spurred his horse and galloped ahead. The driver became impatient. "Are you coming?" he asked. The escort's riderless horse trotted by the wagon out of the darkness. "It's about time. We need to . . ." The driver paused as the horse continued past him. He yelled at the remaining escort, "Boaz, get your gun."

"For what? The fool probably fell off his horse trying to get that stray," Boaz replied.

Tick, click.

The driver froze at the sound of a cocking revolver from the other side of the wagon.

Then a voice called, "Drop the reins!"

The driver pulled his revolver and yelled at Boaz, "Get back to headquarters! Tell 'em we're ambushed!" He spun around and aimed into the darkness.

Bam!

The driver's hand flung sideways as his revolver flew out of his grip. He fell onto the wagon seat, holding his hand. Boaz spurred his mount and raced toward the mountains. Noah emerged from the other side of the wagon and aimed his revolver at the fleeing man. Boaz charged through the grass and disappeared into the darkness. Noah kicked the dirt and holstered his revolver. He approached the wagon as Fern forced the driver to the ground.

"I thought you had that second escort!" Noah yelled at Fern.

"I did until you let go of the first escort's horse and it nearly trampled me!"

"What was I supposed to do? With Kiyiya watching our horses, I had to get to the wagon."

"Did the third guy get away?" Fern asked.

"Yeah, I couldn't get a shot off." Noah stood over the wounded driver. "If you think that hand hurts, a leg is unbearable." He pulled his revolver and aimed at the driver's thigh. "I heard you tell your buddy to go to headquarters. What else are you going to tell us? And I am not asking twice." He pulled the hammer back.

"Look, I'm just a hired driver. Those men are the ones you want. I had nothing to do with any of this!"

"Then why pull a gun on me?" Noah buried his knee into the man's chest and aimed the barrel under his chin.

"Okay! What do you want?"

"What's in the crate?" Noah asked.

"Wolves from the preserve. We are helping to remove them from . . ."

"Don't lie to me!" Noah yelled and pressed his knee farther into the man's chest. "Where are you taking them?"

"Frederick. The train depot. We ship them to Texas," the man said.

"Where in Texas?"

"To a ranch. They breed them there."

"Don't give me that nonsense!" Noah said. "You hunt them for sport, don't you? You're making money off the killing of these wolves." The man remained silent. "Mister, don't make me break a promise."

Fern stepped near Noah and pressed on his shoulder. "Easy." He knelt next to the man as Kiyiya arrived with the horses. "Why don't you spare us all the trouble and tell us what kind of wolves and how many of them are in the crates?"

Observing Noah's rage, the driver surrendered any hope for resistance. "Red wolves. There are four of them. The wolves down south are hunted out. We are doing the preserve a favor. They want the wolves dead anyway. We're just giving them a place to go."

"And die!" Noah replied. "Who is your distributor?"

"Some guy from out West. A Hamilton somebody."

"Ellis Hamilton?" Noah asked.

"Yeah. It's his shipping company. He owns the ranch in Texas too," the driver said.

Noah backed away from the driver as Fern questioned him. "Do you know that guy?"

"Yes. And you should too. He was the owner of that store back in Dodge City. He was the one on that supply train to Adobe Walls. He tried to kill me. Kiyiya saved me from him."

Fern searched the driver. He pulled several folded papers from his pockets. He checked the wagon and found a binder with more papers. Using a lantern from the wagon, he reviewed the binder and read the papers.

"Noah, come here." Noah approached Fern, still glaring at the wounded driver on the ground. "Look at this." Fern handed Noah a drawing.

"This is the map Rebecca made," Noah said.

"Check this one."

Noah took the paper and gasped at the drawing. "Kiyiya, what does this look like to you?"

Kiyiya stepped into the light and studied the document. "That is the road to my house."

"Look here," Fern said. "It has the number four by the barn."

"They know about the wolf pups," Noah said. He stormed toward the driver.

"Noah!" Kiyiya yelled. Noah stopped. "No." Noah backed away from the driver and tended to the horses.

Fern knelt by the driver. "What do you know about these wolf pups?"

The driver suffered through the pain in his hand. "They have other men watching the house and barn. They plan to take them tomorrow and ship them to Texas with the rest of the wolves."

"What do you do with the wolves after you kill them?" Fern asked.

"We sell the hides, or the hunters keep them. This special breed is worth a lot."

Fern felt distress and leaned against the wagon. The driver's details about the wolves concerned him. He listened to the wolves whine inside the crate behind him. He wondered about the next move of their developing plan. Against his better judgment, he yelled at Noah for advisement.

"What should we do with him?" Fern asked.

Noah handed the reins to Kiyiya. "What I did with the others." He pulled his revolver and spun it. In a wide movement, he swung the heel of the weapon into the side of the driver's head. The impact rendered him unconscious. "Why would you ask that? You know what we're doing."

"No, I don't. I don't have a clue what we are doing," Fern said. "Look around you, Noah. We have a crate full of rare wolves everyone is interested in. That escaped escort is racing back to headquarters to let his buddies know what has happened to their quarry. And there isn't a safe place anywhere in this territory to take these wolves! Is that convincing enough for you?"

Noah stared at the unconscious driver and then looked at the large crate strapped to the wagon. He shrugged at the overwhelming problems Fern described. Surrendering to the complexity of the moment, he relied on his experience with similar situations and chose desperation. He spun his revolver several times and landed it squarely in the holster. He faced Fern with hidden doubt, knowing he had no idea what to do next.

"We got what we came for. We need to finish it," Noah said. He addressed Kiyiya. "Fern is right. He and I will handle all of that. You must get home and warn Rebecca. Make sure Mayuri is safe and hide those wolves at Fern's ranch. That is the last place they will look until we can do something about them." Noah took the binder and wrote on a page. He ripped it from the binder and folded it. "Give this to Rebecca. Tell her it is important and that she must do this right away."

Kiyiya took the note and said, "I will. What about my wolves in that crate?"

"I'll take care of them." He extended his hand with an odd sense of farewell. "Thank you for what you did for me at Adobe Walls. And most of all, thank you for helping me change."

"Remember who gives you strength." Kiyiya climbed onto the saddle and disappeared into the darkness.

"Touching," Fern said. "But you have no idea what we're doing, do you?"

"Of course I do," Noah said. "We are stealing this wagon full of crated rare wolves and getting out of here."

"And going where? You know that once they find out these wolves didn't show up at the Frederick train depot, they will cover the entire area looking for them."

"Then I guess that rules out Frederick," Noah replied.

"I should have left with Kiyiya." He mounted his horse. "All right, get that desperate look off your face and lead the way. But remember, if you get me in a gunfight, I'm shooting you first."

"You worry too much," Noah said and climbed on the wagon. He grabbed the reins and steered the team around. "Besides, what did you tell me a long time ago? Something about finding a purpose? Well, here we are."

"I said *your* purpose. That had nothing to do with me!" Fern said. "What was that you wrote and gave to Kiyiya?"

"A backup plan. I'll tell you when this is over. That way, if this doesn't work, you will never know."

"You are like a bad bet with cold cards. And to think I thought I missed you all these years." Fern urged his mount forward as they journeyed into the darkness.

CHAPTER 11

October 1907

Boaz navigated the terrain with daring acuity. He guided his horse at a steady trot to make time and avoid hidden obstacles in the darkness. The night had hours remaining as he squinted to see the ground ahead. Keeping to the valley grasses, he used the dim starlight to traverse the area and locate a solitary lantern burning brightly in a cove. He succumbed to relief and steered his mount toward the light. Large tents were pitched under a canopy of trees. He dismounted near the middle tent and rushed through the opening.

"What are you doing here?" a voice from behind him asked. "You're supposed to be leading that wagon to the Frederick depot."

"Dutch! We got ambushed. We were on the way there when two men jumped us. I think I'm the only one who escaped. For all I know, the rest of them are dead."

"Did you see the men who ambushed you?" Dutch asked.

"It was dark. I was with the wagon when the driver got his gun shot out of his hand. It was an impossible shot. I rode away after that."

The tent flap was flung open. A tall man emerged with a lantern. He held the light high to see the faces of the two men. "What did you say?"

"Mr. Hamilton, I was with the wagon, and we got ambushed, and . . ."

"No! After that. The man who fired that impossible shot. What did he look like?"

Boaz became nervous. "Well, sir, it was dark, and he was on the other side of the wagon. I couldn't make him out. I heard his voice, but that was it. It all happened so fast."

Ellis Hamilton limped closer toward Boaz. "Did anyone see this man? He had to be close enough to fire a shot like that in the dark. Someone had to have seen him."

Boaz stepped back. "No, sir. I don't even think the driver saw him. The man was pretty far away from us."

"Hmm. That's a pity. And to think I hired capable men to deal with a situation like that. Or better yet, avoid a situation like that altogether."

Boaz took a deep breath and avoided eye contact with Ellis.

Dutch approached Ellis. "What? Do you think you know who that was?"

Ellis recalled his past. "I knew a man who could shoot like that a long time ago."

"Do you think it was him?"

"No. The man I'm thinking of is dead." Ellis spoke to Boaz. "Did they take the wagon?" Boaz nodded. "And my special-breed wolves?" Boaz remained still. "I see." Ellis jabbed his finger in Boaz's chest. "Round up every man you can find and get back out there. Send word to the Frederick depot to watch for them. You find my wagon. Those are my wolves. I want them back. Alive."

"Yes, Mr. Hamilton." Boaz said.

"Dutch," Ellis said. "Have Trey Doyle come to my tent." Ellis hobbled back to his canvas dwelling and placed the lantern on a stand. He grimaced from the occasional pain radiating through his leg. He rubbed the soreness and guzzled from his canteen.

Trey parted the tent flap and passed through to see Ellis lying on a cot. Ellis twirled a revolver while staring at the top of the tent. Trey rubbed the sleep from his eyes and pulled a chair near the cot. Ellis remained silent for several seconds, twirling his revolver. He held the weapon near his chest and kept his focus on the canvas.

"Seems we have other parties interested in our work," Ellis said.

"Boaz only told me some of what happened. They got ambushed?" Trey asked.

Ellis rolled to his side. "Who ambushes a bunch of wolves no one knew about?" Trey raised his eyebrows in search of an answer. "Not to mention the money and resources I am spending to get those wolves out of here nice and quiet like. Or, what was it you said? My wolves would be halfway to Texas before anyone would even know what happened?" Ellis sent a fiery stare at Trey. "And now that idiot comes riding in here, telling me my wolves, my rig, and a number of my highly paid escorts have been dispersed by some phantom gunman in the night!" Ellis raised his revolver at Trey and locked the hammer back. "I do not recall this being included in your foolproof plan, Mr. Doyle."

"All right," Trey said. "I'm as surprised as you are."

Ellis swung his legs off the cot and lunged at Trey. He shoved him backward in the chair. Trey slammed against the ground as Ellis stood over him. "*Surprised* is hardly the word I would expect from a so-called expert I paid handsomely to put on staff here! Get up!" Trey rubbed his head and stood. "Obviously, the plan has changed. I will keep it simple for you this time. I want to know what you are going to do about my wolves. As I expect you know, they are a considerable investment for me."

"It must be Rebecca and that new guy who arrived recently. They are the only ones who know. I took all the information from her report," Trey said.

Ellis sat on his cot. "What new guy? I thought you had everyone cleared through my contact with the senior members."

"I did. This guy showed up out of nowhere. Someone else hired him."

"Who is he?" Ellis asked.

"Noah Wrath. He came from Yellowstone. From what I could gather, he is friends with a rancher from Cache named Fernando Raul."

Ellis squinted with a sinister countenance. "Noah Wrath."

"Do you know him?" Trey asked.

Ellis ignored his question. "That explains the impossible shot. This complicates things even further."

"Hardly," Trey said. "If they took the wolves, it's obvious they are trying to save them. My guess is they will hide them at Raul's ranch. I'll send some men there at first light."

"What about those wolf pups at that Comanche's barn?" Ellis asked. "Those pups are part of our agreement if you expect to get paid for this."

"I have some men who have been watching the place for a while. They know what to do."

"You put a lot of faith in your men, Trey. So far, I'm not impressed."

"Look, after the buffalo arrive, I'll go to headquarters in the morning and see what I can find out. There are only so many places around here where they can hide a bunch of wolves without my men or someone else seeing them. We will get them back," Trey said.

"What about the return of those buffalo later today? You are going to have every dignitary and local citizen for miles attending that event," Ellis said. "It could draw attention I do not need."

"I'll take care of it. They would be crazy to bring them within miles of the preserve with those buffalo arriving. The event will work to our favor anyway. With everyone there, it will be easier for my men to find the wolves without interference."

Ellis was unconvinced of Trey's evolving plan. "You are running out of time and costing me money. This entire plan of yours has become a liability. If those wolves are not at the Frederick depot by noon—"

"They will be there!" Trey said. Then he charged out of the tent and disappeared into the darkness.

Kiyiya shuddered awake. He sat up from the grass and panicked. The morning sunlight blinded him as he struggled to remember. His horse fed from a nearby tree. He watched the animal and checked his surroundings. The Wichita Mountains towered behind the contoured foothills of Fort Sill. Birds chirped their eager acknowledgment as Kiyiya rubbed his aching shoulder. A morning breeze lumbered through the meadow and across his tired face. Its gentle passing was followed by the revelation of his awakened memory.

"Mayuri!"

The burst of adrenaline motivated him through the stiffness and cracking of his aged joints. He came to his feet and hurried to his horse. He got on the saddle and raced home.

The previous night's trek had brought him closer to his house than he had realized. He dashed to the opening of his barn and dismounted in slow stride. The momentum caused him to tumble through the open barn doors and collide with a pile of hay. He dusted off and scrambled to his feet.

He raised his head to see a revolver in his face.

"Heck of an entrance, old man. It nearly got you shot."

A man wearing a black cowboy hat and dark beard forced Kiyiya against the wall. He looked at Kiyiya with contempt and yelled to his side, "You found those wolf pups yet?"

"No," another man replied from the other side of the barn.

The man pressed the revolver into Kiyiya's chest. "I know who you are. We've been watching you. Been watching that little granddaughter of yours too. Unless you want this to get real ugly, why don't you show us where those wolves are." Kiyiya remained silent. The man smirked at him and spit from his wad of chewing tobacco. "Hey! That little girl across the street. Her parents are at work by now, right?"

"Yeah," the other man replied.

The man frowned at Kiyiya. "She should be coming over for Grandpa to babysit anytime now. Maybe she can get you to talk." He seized Kiyiya by the collar and threw him into the hay. "Or, maybe I can get her to talk." The man cocked the hammer and aimed at Kiyiya. "Where are the wolves?"

Knock, knock, knock.

Both men looked at the opposite barn door. The bearded man grabbed Kiyiya and pulled him up as the other man rushed to the side of the door and pulled his revolver. "Answer," the man ordered Kiyiya.

The Comanche cleared his throat, then said, "Who is it?"

"Mayuri."

The man held his revolver near Kiyiya's side. "Tell her to come in."

Kiyiya expressed confusion at the unfamiliar sound of Mayuri's voice. Before he could speak, the strange voice outside responded again. "Come quick!"

The man looked at his counterpart near the door, "Open the door and pull her in here!"

The other man holstered his revolver and opened the door. Seeing no one, he stepped outside. The back end of a shovel slammed into his unsuspecting face. His nose and jaw cracked from the impact as he hit the barn wall and collapsed on the ground.

"What's going on?" the man with Kiyiya yelled. Hearing no reply, he forced Kiyiya toward the door. They approached as Cecilia stepped in front of the opening with a shovel in her hands.

"Drop your gun!" A voice demanded from behind them. The man saw Rebecca aiming her revolver. "Now!"

"You women are asking for it," the man said with a sneer. He pulled Kiyiya next to him and angled between Rebecca and Cecilia. He aimed his revolver at Cecilia. "Ain't much you can do with a shovel."

Cecilia dropped the shovel and grabbed a rifle that was leaning against the barn wall. She cocked the lever, aimed at the man, and asked, "How about this?"

The man backed farther into the barn. He pressed his revolver into Kiyiya's ribs. "I'm getting out of here. If you want this old man to survive, you had better get out of my way." He stopped near a boarded crate covered in burlap sacks and hay. "I mean it!"

Grrr!

The man spun around at the growl behind him. He looked down at the burlap sacks draped over the dark crate opening. "There they are."

"Tseena!" Kiyiya yelled and shoved the man sideways.

A large red wolf lunged from underneath the burlap cover and slammed into the man's thigh. She buried her jagged fangs into his thigh and attacked with a relentless frenzy. The man stumbled from the attack and fell to the ground. The wolf ripped and tore at his clothes as he raised his revolver.

"No!" Kiyiya yelled. He swung his leg forward and kicked the revolver out of the man's hand. The weapon hit the wall and bounced within his reach. He rolled to his side and slammed his boot into the wolf. She whimpered in pain and released him. Dazed from the hit, the wolf limped back to the crate and fell in front of the opening. Four wolf pups emerged from the crate and surrounded their injured mother.

The man saw the pups and sneered at Kiyiya in defiance. "Those wolves are coming with me!" He stretched across the ground and reached for his revolver. The heel of a large cowhide leather boot crushed the man's hand against the weapon. "Ah!" he yelled, then looked up to see the barrel of another revolver aimed at his head. The distinctive click of the hammer resonated in his ears.

"No. *You* are coming with me." The man shifted his focus to see a bright silver badge glistening on the vest of Sheriff Louis Cassidy. The sheriff continued to press his boot heel firmly across the man's knuckles and kicked the weapon away from his grasp. "Mister, you move an inch, and I'll have that lady over there bury you with that shovel. Do you hear me?"

The man relented as Sheriff Cassidy rolled him over and handcuffed him. Dee Cassidy appeared from the side of the barn and walked next to the sheriff. She noticed the scene and waved at Cecilia. "Who needs a shovel when your husband is the sheriff?"

"Fine time for you two to show up!" Cecilia said. "What took you so long? Did you get my telegram?"

"I told you we would be back today," Dee replied and picked up the man's revolver. "It's a good thing we took the early train back to Cache. It is so crowded at the depot with those buffalo arriving today."

Sheriff Cassidy stood over the cuffed man. "What in the world happened here? And who is that lying over there in the dirt? He's not dead, is he?"

Rebecca joined the group as Kiyiya and Cecilia gathered with them. Cecilia looked at the unconscious man by the door. "He'll live. Might be short a few teeth, though. His face dented my shovel."

"Looks like you made a fine mess of things," Dee jeered.

Cecilia warned her sister. "Don't make me lock you in the closet again."

Sheriff Cassidy rolled his eyes at the two sisters and addressed Rebecca. "Ms. McGovern, I hope you can provide some explanation for all of this. I think my sister-in-law has more than covered the shovel details."

Rebecca stared at the wolf pups lying next to their injured mother. She approached the wolf with Kiyiya and triaged the wound. "Those men were trying to steal these wolves. Cecilia and I had to hurry and come up with a plan to protect the wolves. We knew if we could catch those men in the act, we could arrest them. It was going well until Kiyiya arrived. He didn't know what was happening and rode into the middle of everything. Things got a bit out of control after that. I'm very glad you showed up. Thank you."

Sheriff Cassidy helped the handcuffed man to his feet. "Poachers, huh? I guess we can add that to the list of charges to be filed against you and your friend over there."

"You don't have nothing on me!" the man yelled.

Sheriff Cassidy tightened his grip on the man's arm. "I think I'll have plenty of time to figure that out while you wait in my jail for the judge to come back next month." He looked at Kiyiya. "Are you okay? That was quite an effort I saw." Kiyiya gave his appreciation. "Good. I will need statements from all of you. Don't wander off too far." He pulled the man forward. "Come on. Let's get your friend over there ready to join you."

Kiyiya watched the man stumble by and rushed to the women. "Where is Mayuri? Is she safe?"

"Oh, yes," Cecilia replied. "She is with her parents at our ranch. I'm sure you knew that was not Mayuri's voice at the door. I had to lure him over somehow."

The relieved group tended to the wolves. Rebecca examined the wolf. "She appears to be okay. Maybe some rib pain. I have some medications at the headquarters I can treat her with."

They gathered the pups in the crate and walked out of the barn. Rebecca looked around the area. "Where are Noah and Fern? They didn't come with you?" she asked Kiyiya.

"No. They had to . . ." his eyes widened from memory. "Wait, I forgot." He dug in his pocket. "Here. This is from Noah." He handed her a folded paper.

Her curiosity peaked as she read the note. Seconds passed before panic ensued. "Oh no." She faced Cecilia and Dee with an anxious plea. "I need your help!"

The morning sun breached the horizon with full brilliance, casting its rays upon the grass-covered plains. Visitors from across Oklahoma Territory—settlers, ranchers, and people of several tribes—gathered near the Wichita National Forest and Game Preserve holding pens. A contagious enthusiasm permeated the assembled crowd. Many onlookers wore their best attire in celebration of the long-awaited day.

The return of the buffalo to Oklahoma Territory had finally arrived. Preserve staff scurried among the wagons, crates, and fences, ensuring an error-free event. Newspaper reporters worked the scene to capture every historic detail. People of local tribes stood by the fences, waiting for the release of the buffalo. The moment brought joy, united with stories of tribal pasts. Elder tribesmen and generations of families shared the symbiotic relationship between the buffalo and their ancestors with the younger onlookers.

The long train ride from New York ended at the Cache depot. The final stretch of the journey was by wagon to the preserve. The rigs rolled into position with large crates containing the weary buffalo. The crowd became more anxious, waiting to see the great beasts lumber from confinement and trod again upon their native ground.

Noah watched the spectacle. He wore his cowboy hat low over his brow to avoid detection. He noticed the preserve staff diligently preparing for the buffalo's release. Horses and wagons continued to arrive with more people, who were gathering to watch the historic event. A lone horseman departed the crowd and galloped across the prairie, away from the holding pens. Noah backed his mount down the slope and out of sight. He stood in the stirrups and watched the rider.

"Trey Doyle," he mumbled. "Now where are you off to?" He urged his mount forward and followed Trey. He kept his distance and gauged Trey's direction. Confident in his destination, Noah flanked Trey's route and coaxed his mount to the preserve headquarters.

Trey tied his horse's reins and approached the headquarters door. A rider raced toward him from the field and pulled his mount to an abrupt stop. He wiped the dust from his face and addressed Trey.

"I've got men on every road leading to Cache from the preserve. I'm waiting to hear back from the men at the Comanche's house. I'll let you know as soon as they arrive."

"Good work, Boaz," Trey replied. "Think of places they could be hiding those wolves. They will be desperate. What about the Raul ranch?"

"The men are in place there."

"Okay. Don't wander off too far and keep an eye out. I'll be out shortly."

Trey opened the front door of the headquarters. He stepped inside and hung his cowboy hat on the rack. He saw Noah standing behind the door. Noah lunged at Trey and grabbed him by the collar with both hands. He thrust Trey against the wall and pinned him upright.

"How's this for desperate?" Noah asked, then slammed his fist across Trey's face. The impact jolted his jaw as he slid to the floor, unconscious.

Noah hurried to the back of the building and flung the door open. Fern stood on the wagon, feeding the wolves through an opening in the crate. He jumped down and wiped his hands.

"I assume our friend in there is compromised," Fern said. Noah ignored him and looked around the back of the building. "I can see the next part of your plan is still in question. What do we do next? Or should I even ask? Once they finish delivering those buffalo to the holding pens, the entire preserve staff will be on their way back here."

"Would you shut up for a minute! I'm trying to think," Noah said.

"Well, think faster! Those stinking dogs over there are driving me nuts with their barking," Fern said. "They are going to attract everyone to us if we don't get out of here."

Noah saw the kenneled German shepherds. The dogs growled and barked at them. He grabbed some of the food and pitched it in the kennels. The wailing canines focused their attention on the food and began to whine. "Put all that food on the wagon and drive it over here."

"Why?" Fern asked.

Noah pitched the food in the kennel. "Insurance."

Boaz sat upon his mount from the elevated position of a hill. The Wichita Mountains bordered either side of him, providing an advantageous view. A wagon departed from behind the headquarters and headed for the buffalo holding pens. He watched it follow a different route away from the main dirt road. Its rapid speed caught his attention as two horsemen rode to the front of the headquarters. Confused, Boaz urged his horse to a quick gallop. He arrived at the headquarters to see Ellis Hamilton and Dutch.

"Where is Trey?" Ellis asked.

"Inside when I last saw him. Unless he left with that wagon a few minutes ago," Boaz replied.

"What wagon?" Ellis asked. "Open that door."

Dutch entered the building with Ellis and Boaz. "No one's here."

"Uhh."

All three men looked at the floor to see Trey moaning and rubbing his jaw.

"What happened to you?" Dutch asked. Boaz helped Trey to his feet and guided him into a chair.

"Where is he?" Trey asked.

"Who?" Boaz inquired.

"Noah Wrath. He knocked me out."

"When did this happen?" Dutch asked.

"When I got here this morning. My head is killing me."

Ellis walked next to Trey. "I give you another opportunity to succeed, and this is what you do with it? You had Wrath in this building, and you let him get away?"

"He blindsided me!" Trey yelled. "I didn't know he was here. It makes no sense that he would be here in the first place."

"Was the wagon with him?" Dutch asked.

"I said I don't know," Trey replied.

"I saw a wagon leave before you two arrived," Boaz said. "I thought it might have been Trey and he didn't tell me."

Dutch spoke to Ellis. "He brought the wolves here."

Ellis sneered at Boaz. He contemplated the information with shrinking patience. "What direction did you see this wagon going?"

"East. Toward the buffalo holding pens," Boaz replied.

The room became silent as each man debated his thoughts for a reasonable answer. "Why would he go there?" Dutch asked. "The place is crawling with people. They will see those wolves for sure."

Ellis focused on Trey. "If you stay here, you can find another job. Otherwise, get up." Trey rubbed his jaw. "All of you, get on your horses. You!" Ellis yelled at Boaz. "Take us to that wagon."

The four men motivated their mounts and dashed across the grasslands. The buffalo holding pens became visible. The men noticed the dwindled population of onlookers and rode to the gathering of preserve staff near the gate. They tied their mounts and infiltrated the group of overseers. They approached the pens and saw seven buffalo standing together.

Ellis spoke to one of the operators. "Did all the buffalo arrive?"

The operator was busy writing on a clipboard. "Yes. The first shipment is finished."

"What do you mean the first shipment?" Ellis asked.

"The buffalo. They are arriving in two shipments from the Cache depot. There are fifteen total. We are getting the arrival time of the remaining eight. Should be any time now."

Ellis looked around the area. "Have you seen a wagon hauling a large wooden crate come through here today?"

"Just the wagons hauling the buffalo crates." Ellis became frustrated as the operator looked up from his clipboard. "We did have an extra wagon join the caravan back to Cache, though. Not sure who it was. Come to think of it, they were hauling a crate. But there were several folks heading back to Cache."

"How long ago did they leave?"

"The event ended about ten minutes ago. They shouldn't be too far ahead," the operator replied.

Ellis limped back to the waiting men. "Seems our counterparts are smarter than I thought. They are hiding in the crowd and trying to get back to Cache. Most likely that ranch you were talking about. Do you know a faster way there?"

"No. This is the only road. But their wagon is slow," Trey replied. "Come on."

They galloped away in pursuit of the wagon train. Several horses, buggies, and wagons lined the road, returning from the buffalo arrival. The men navigated the traffic, desperate to get through the congestion.

"Look! Up ahead at that fork in the road," Dutch said.

A wagon with a large wooden crate strapped to it was stopped on the roadside. The men urged their horses forward. The wagon driver noticed their speedy pursuit and snapped the reins across the team. The horses jumped to attention and ran ahead. The driver pulled a bandanna over his nose and mouth. He steered the team away from the dense traffic and took the right-side fork in the road.

"He saw us!" Trey yelled. "Boaz, ride to the left of him. I'll cut him off on the right and stop the team."

All four men surrounded the wagon. Boaz and Trey reached for the team and struggled to slow their advance. The masked driver reached for a whip and cracked it above Trey's head. Trey grabbed the saddle horn and stopped his fall. The wagon and four pursuers rushed down the dirt road as the driver continued to urge the team faster.

Dutch pulled his revolver and rode next to the wagon. He aimed at the driver, shouting, "Stop this rig now!" The masked driver noticed the weapon and pulled on the reins. The horses heaved and halted their advance. The driver steered the team to the side, near several houses that lined the dirt road. The four men encircled the wagon, with Dutch keeping his revolver aimed at the driver. "Get off that wagon!"

Ellis rode near the driver, who was now standing on the ground, and asked, "What is with the bandanna?" The driver remained silent with his hands up. "Pull that off him."

Dutch reached over and yanked the cloth down to reveal the smiling face of Fernando Raul. "Who are you?" Dutch asked.

"Just a local out for a ride," Fern said.

"How about I make you talk," Dutch said and aimed his revolver at Fern's chest.

"You are standing in the middle of this neighborhood. There are people nearby. You wouldn't want to shoot that thing and make a scene now, would you?"

The men listened as whining and clawing sounds emanated from the crate. The noises began to intensify as Trey dismounted.

"We know what you have in the crate," he said. "Those wolves belong to us. Back away from the wagon." Trey signaled to Boaz. "Drive the wagon. I'll get your mount. Let's get out of here."

"What about him?" Dutch asked.

Trey looked around the area as various people began to gather in their yards. "Leave him. We don't need a scene."

Fern began to back away from the men as the whining became barking. Trey looked at the crate. "Boaz, open the slot on that crate."

Boaz jumped from the seat and landed next to the crate. The barking became more intense. He opened the slot and peered inside. "Trey, you need to see this."

Trey climbed on the wagon and looked inside the crate. Two German shepherds clawed at the wooden sides at the sight of their owner. "What? Those are my dogs! How did you . . ."

"That's enough, boys," Fern said as he held his revolver in his outstretched arm.

"There are four of us, mister," Dutch said.

"Just more for me to shoot at," Fern replied. "Don't think for a second that I won't blow a hole through as many of you as I can." He watched the hands of each man and backed to the nearest yard.

"I say we shoot him," Dutch said.

"All of you, shut up," Ellis said. He looked at Trey. "You ignorant fool. Don't you see what he is doing? He is stalling us. He switched the wolves for your stupid dogs!" Ellis faced Fern. "This isn't over." He ordered the men. "Mount up."

"By the way!" Fern yelled at Ellis. "My friend wanted to know how that limp of yours is doing."

Ellis ignored Fern as Trey calmed his German shepherds and asked, "Ellis, what about my dogs?"

Ellis pulled out his revolver and shot at the crate. The round impacted at the corner, splintering the wood. "I'd better not see you or your worthless dogs again." He aimed the revolver at Dutch and Boaz. "You two, come with me."

Ellis and the men rode away as Fern stepped near the wagon and said, "Toss your revolver on the road."

Trey stared at Fern in defeat. "You can't do anything to me. I'm a staff member of the preserve, and these are my dogs."

Fern climbed on the wagon. "I'll remember that when the time comes. Get up here and drive this rig."

"What are you talking about?"

"You'll see." Fern directed Trey to the driver's seat and stood behind him with his revolver drawn. "Get moving."

Ellis and the men arrived near the Cache train depot. They maintained a casual appearance in the crowd to avoid attention. They trotted along the road and stopped near the wagons carrying the empty buffalo crates. The rigs waited in line near the station. Ellis dismounted and directed Dutch and Boaz to follow.

"Split up. Check those buffalo crates," Ellis said. "If you see my wolves, take over the wagon and drive it to Frederick. I'll have another team meet you along the way. Stay away from town and try not to be seen."

"What do we say if someone sees us?" Boaz asked.

"Nothing. Tell them you are with the preserve."

The men dispersed and began checking the wagons. People had lined the depot in preparation for the next arrival of buffalo. One train readied for departure. The steam whistle sounded its impending departure as the conductor made his rounds. The men searched the wagons and eventually came to the last rig in line. Dutch climbed on the wagon and noticed two crates strapped together. He looked between the slats of the first crate. Four red wolves rested quietly in beds of hay.

He waved at Ellis and Boaz, then pointed at the crate. Ellis mounted his horse as Boaz rushed to the wagon and joined Dutch. He steered the wagon out of line as Ellis led them forward. He looked back to see the side of the second crate burst open. Four armed officers rushed out of it with their rifles aimed at Dutch and Boaz. The stunned men raised their arms in the air as two of the officers stopped the rig. Ellis watched the scene unfold. He spurred his horse to advance.

"Ellis Hamilton, I presume?" a rider yelled, blocking his escape route. Ellis noticed John Bruce in front of him.

He pulled his revolver and aimed at John. "Get out of my way!" He cocked the hammer.

Bam!

A round impacted the revolver, flinging it away from Ellis' hand. The force of the shot knocked him from his saddle. He fell hard against the ground, holding his bloody hand. Then he gained his breath and rolled to find his weapon. He looked up to see Sheriff Louis Cassidy holding his revolver.

"That was quite a shot," Sheriff Cassidy said and knelt next to Ellis. "Can't say I have ever seen a shot like that before." He directed his attention to an open railcar. Ellis grimaced in pain as he saw Noah holster his revolver in the doorway.

"Those are my wolves!" Ellis shouted.

"Those wolves are under the protection of the United States government," John said. "And you, sir, are facing federal charges of poaching on a government preserve and transporting federally protected wildlife with government equipment." John knelt next to Ellis. "Those were never your wolves."

"We will see what the senior members say about this! I know who you are," Ellis countered. "I am under contract, which means the government has no say in this matter. You're just a pawn."

"If you did know me, then you would know that the senior member who sponsored you was arrested for contract fraud." He leaned closer to Ellis. "I took his place. I am a senior member now. And you are going away for a long time. Sheriff, get these vermin out of my sight."

Sheriff Cassidy helped Ellis to his feet. Ellis watched as the wagon was backed to the open railcar and the crated wolves were loaded on the train. The whistle blew a final time as the train lurched forward. The railcar door began to close as Noah leaned out. Ellis watched him as Noah yelled, "You lose!" and tapped the side of his leg. John snickered at Noah's gesture and tipped his cowboy hat. Noah leaned against the wolf crate and waved as the railcar door closed.

"Good work, Sheriff. Thank you for the quick response. This was all rather sudden, from what I gather," John said.

"Glad to be of service and to finally get rid of these gentlemen. We will hold them until the federal marshal arrives from Oklahoma City," Sheriff Cassidy replied. His deputies marched Dutch and

Boaz by in handcuffs. A wagon with escort riders rushed through the crowd. The sheriff looked to see Cecilia and Dee driving the rig. "Something tells me this is not over yet."

Rebecca tied her horse and ran to John. "What happened? We came as fast as we could. Fern came back to the ranch to let us know about the wolves. He has Trey tied up in the back of the wagon over there."

John strolled by the wagon and said, "Trey Doyle. I remember you. It has been a while. It appears you continue to be the nuisance you were the first time you worked for me. This is twice I have fired you. There will not be a third." John asked for Sheriff Cassidy, who cuffed Trey and took him away.

John spoke to Rebecca. "You did well. Are you okay after all of that? You have had quite an experience."

"I'm fine, Dad." Rebecca looked around the area. "Where are Noah and the wolves?"

"I'm afraid you are too late. When I got your message from Noah, all I had to work with was this one train departure. We couldn't wait, and the agreement was to get the wolves out of here as soon as possible. Someone had to ride as escort with the wolves. The crate cannot ship alone. Noah was the best alternative and, frankly, the only answer we had," John replied. "It took some effort with the tight timeline, but I was able to pay for transportation and get the right connections for delivery. The train could not wait any longer."

Rebecca stared ahead at the desolate train track. "Delivery to where?" she asked.

CHAPTER 12

December 1907

The week of Christmas brought more snow to the varying elevations of Yellowstone National Park. The region was blanketed by fresh powder. Cold-climate creatures migrated in search of scarce meals. A herd of buffalo roamed the riverbanks for remaining grasses. The beckoning howl of a wolf echoed across the valley. Its remote call gave alert to the changing seasons. The annual test of strength and endurance for the Yellowstone occupants was upon them. Another hard winter was about to begin.

Noah remained prone at the foot of a snowbank. He kept still and watched the darkened tree line. The snow partially covered his body, allowing his face to be seen. The steam from his breath rose in short wisps before dissipating in the freezing wind. Several minutes passed without action. Surrendering to another failed lesson to teach the young wolf, Noah slowly raised his head from the snow.

A wet tongue smeared upward along his exposed cheek.

"Ugh." Noah saw a red wolf patiently staring at him. He sat by the wolf. It watched Noah without movement. "Okay, come here." Overjoyed, the red wolf bounded on his lap and licked under his chin. "I think you've finally learned the secret to stalking, Kiyiya." He rubbed the wolf behind the ears. "Come on. Let's go warm up."

Noah trekked through the snow with the young wolf bounding in front of him. They crossed a snow-covered meadow and journeyed through a section of forest. Pushing through another snowbank, they saw a column of smoke rising from the rock chimney of an expanded cabin. Four more rooms had been added to the dwelling, providing more amenities and comforts.

Noah waved at two people who were stacking firewood in front of the cabin. The essential fuel had been piled high along the log walls. The red wolf perked its ears at the sight of three more red wolves resting near a fire. Noah saw the wintry scene with tranquil pleasure. The abundance of nature was captured in the moment. The recent freedom of the red wolves within the expansive landscape of Yellowstone provided new hope for all of them. The success of the Wichita Mountains endeavor was visible. He thought of his purpose fulfilled as he watched the red wolves thrive. He hoped that one day, the red wolves could return to their native Oklahoma. Reuniting with Kai had filled the tender void left by Kiyiya. He missed his abundant wisdom. The influence of his Comanche friend resonated in his soul. For the first time in his life, Noah felt peace.

Grrr.

The red wolf spun around to see Japheth standing at the tree line behind them. Noah saw his companion glaring at the red wolf. Japheth lowered his head and approached the red wolf with a stalking presence.

"Do you see that, Kiyiya? That is how it's done," Noah said.

The red wolf ignored Noah and jumped playfully at Japheth. Standing twice the size and weight of the red wolf, Japheth wanted nothing to do with the naive youngster. Japheth towered over the lesser red wolf and snapped an intimidating warning. The adolescent whined at the sight of fangs and scurried to the cabin.

Noah chuckled at his resentful counterpart and called to Japheth. "Easy, my friend. In time, you will learn them." He rubbed behind his ears and made eye contact. "And then you will lead them." Japheth nudged him with devoted acknowledgment and stared at the distraught red wolf creeping toward them. Japheth growled again, sending the reluctant red wolf farther away.

"I've spoiled you," Noah said. The daunting predator pawed at him for more attention despite the red wolf whimpering from the fire.

A wagon team emerged from the forest. Noah was relieved to see the weekly supplies arrive as scheduled. He despised having to navigate down the mountain and across the landscape to retrieve sustenance. He trudged through the snow to the wagon as another rig appeared through the woods. He peered across the bright snow to see the distinctive US Army insignia along the wooden railing. Several soldiers off-loaded more supplies and gathered at the rear of the wagon. Noah greeted the team as an officer noticed him.

"By golly, the rumors were true. You're back!" Captain Joseph Hendricks exclaimed. He extended his hand to Noah. "Good to see you, old friend. How was your trip to the plains? Looks like you survived."

"I can't say it was uneventful, but it's good to be back. I see you didn't keep an eye on Kai while I was gone. He ran off and got married!"

"Nia is a sweet woman. Kai did well to marry her," Captain Hendricks said.

"Yes, she is. How have you been?"

"Gaining ground every day. Progress is slow, but we added to our company strength and can spread the wealth with more concentration on the trouble areas. We will get there," Captain Hendricks replied. "Poaching is down considerably, so that is the best news yet. Kai said you have a special breed of wolf you brought back from the Wichita Mountains. How are they faring?"

"They are doing well. They need to adapt to the cold some more, but we will keep feeding them to thicken their winter coats. We hope to start breeding them soon."

"You plan to expand the pack already?" Captain Hendricks asked. Noah acknowledged him. "I'm glad to hear that. Because we caught a poacher crossing into the park, and I brought some more wolves for you." He waved at a sergeant, who lowered a small crate from the wagon and opened the front. Four red wolf pups jumped out across the snow. Each bound buried them nose-deep in the powder.

Noah was stunned. "Where did you find red wolves?"

Captain Hendricks directed his attention to the second rig and walked to the cabin. "Ask her."

Noah saw Rebecca standing by the wagon. His heart raced. Their eyes met with rejuvenation. Noah walked over and stopped in front of her, consumed with joy. She stared at him while he smiled without limitation. A tender grin creased her face as she stepped closer and said, "Hello."

"Hello to you too."

"Because you left Cache so suddenly, you forgot the wolf pups."

"Yes. It's been about three months since then. That was a rather demanding moment," Noah replied. "I admit my attention was focused on some other pressing business. We didn't have long to get the wolves loaded and meet the train departure on time. I'm glad you got my note."

"I know. It wasn't easy trying to find my father under the circumstances. But he told me it managed to work out. You and Fern did well. It was amazing, what you did for those wolves. The preserve owes you a lot."

"Your father? My note said to contact John Bruce and arrange a rail shipment for the wolves Fern and I took from Ellis Hamilton," Noah said.

"Do you mean to tell me that all this time, you never knew that John Bruce is my father?"

"What? You're his daughter?"

She giggled with delight. "I think you've been riding in the dust too long, cowboy. It might be a little musty between your ears."

"Okay, you got me with that one. No, I never knew. I sure hope I never said anything bad about him in front of you," Noah said.

"No, not that I recall. Not many people know anyway. I guess it's a family thing."

"So, is that why you came to Yellowstone? John sent you?" Noah asked.

"Not exactly. I thought I'd escort the wolf pups up here and check out this operation of yours myself. I guess you could say this visit is on my terms, not his."

Noah fixated upon her beauty. His heart pounded from her words. He reached for her hands. "No senior members directed you here to spy on me?"

"No."

"Fern didn't put you up to some crazy scheme of his?"

"Nope."

Noah paused a moment and stared into her eyes. "I missed you," he said.

"I missed you too." Desire overwhelmed them as Rebecca continued. "I couldn't stop thinking about you after you left. It has been difficult for me to love again. I never wanted to. I shut myself off from even the thought of it. But then I met you. And I want so much to give you my heart. That is why I came."

Noah took her in his arms. "Then do it. You already have mine." A tear appeared on her cheek as Noah embraced her with a passionate kiss.

Captain Hendricks passed by. "After you two get reacquainted, my wife and I would like to have you over for dinner this evening." He yelled back at the cabin, "Kai, I expect to see you and Nia too!" He spoke to Noah. "I'm glad Kai finally got married. He is too good a man to not have a sweet woman like Nia to love." He winked at

Rebecca as he walked by. "Of course, Kai is the only good man in these mountains."

She hugged Captain Hendricks. "Thank you, Joseph."

"So, this is the poacher you mentioned?" Noah asked referring to Rebecca.

Captain Hendricks acknowledged him. "If all the poachers looked as beautiful as Rebecca, my wife would start riding shotgun with me on patrols." Captain Hendricks prepared to depart. "I can count on you all for dinner then?"

Noah agreed. "You're the good man in these mountains. Thanks, Captain."

Captain Hendricks tipped his hat to Noah. "And one more thing. Don't bring any of your wolves to dinner! You nearly started a war the last time you did that. That's an order, Wrath."

Noah waved as Captain Hendricks rode away. He held Rebecca close, "Would you like a tour of our humble operation before we leave for dinner?"

Rebecca wrapped her arms around his neck, "Maybe later."

The warming rays of the early-morning sun shone between the thick, wintry clouds drifting above the Wichita Mountains. The buffalo grazed in their holding area upon the preserve. Kiyiya stood nearby, watching the Great Plains giants with rejuvenation of a lifetime of memories. Fern and Cecilia watched from their wagon nearby. Mayuri sat between them, nestled under a blanket that stretched over their laps.

"Grandfather is so happy," she said. "He loves to come here. The buffalo make him feel good. He remembers when he was young with the buffalo."

Cecilia held her close. "Having the buffalo back makes us all happy. This is their home." She looked down at Mayuri. "I saw that you finished your poem. Did you decide on a title for it yet?"

"Yes, I did. Seeing the buffalo return helped me think of a good title. I am going to surprise my grandfather with it tomorrow morning when I read it to him," Mayuri said. "He wants to read it when he wakes up each day."

"I'm sure he will love it," Cecilia said. They watched Kiyiya wait for the sunrise.

"I'm glad he got to keep the injured red wolf. I don't think Kiyiya would have had it any other way," Fern said. "That wolf could not have survived a journey to Yellowstone in its condition. It seems to be healing well."

"This preserve is where Kiyiya belongs," Cecilia said. "And that red wolf with him."

"Why did the wolf pups have to go to Yellowstone?" Mayuri asked.

Fern wrapped his arm around them. "They are safe there. And Noah will protect them."

"Will I ever get to see them again?" Mayuri asked. "Will they get to come home like the buffalo did?"

Fern looked ahead. "I don't know, sweetheart. Maybe someday."

They watched the sun breach the horizon. The brilliant light cast a vibrant glow upon Kiyiya. The red wolf sat by his side. Kiyiya caressed the wolf with affection. Fern, Cecilia, and Mayuri watched in amazement as a large bull buffalo meandered toward the fence. It noticed the wolf and lumbered next to Kiyiya. The trio faced the rising sun with the granite slopes of Mount Scott illuminated behind them.

Cecilia spoke to Fern, "It took so long, and they endured so much. And now they have found peace."

Fern reflected on the treasured scene as a moment born of history. He thought of his many memories of the Great Plains and the endurance of life in the West. Watching the three protagonists stand together, he realized it was not the life he'd lived, but when he'd lived it. Through triumph and tragedy, he'd witnessed the passage of an era. The reign of the Comanche, the domain of the buffalo, and the wandering of the wolf had culminated before him.

As they stood together facing the dawn, Fern said with solemn reverence, "They found refuge."

EPILOGUE

Mayuri's Poem

Where the Mighty Roam

She stood alone near the wired pen,
a sad woman wondering when.
She tried very hard not to cry,
for it was time to say good-bye.
She looked around the tiny fenced lot,
as many bison began to trot.
They gathered together all not knowing,
just what the future would soon be showing.
William T. Hornaday, keeper of the zoo,
approached the woman, with something to do.
"I have someone special for you to meet.
He needs you for a great task to complete."
She wiped her tears and turned to see,
a well-dressed man crouch to a knee.
He noticed her eyes solemn and red,
for he, also, had a tear to shed.
"I'm Franklin S. Rush," and extended his hand.
"I'm building the bison a new home quite grand.
A pleasure to meet you," he grinned with glee.

"But I can tell you're not happy with me."
"I've feared this moment since Mr. Hornaday
said you would come and take the bison away.
The New York Zoo is their place and home.
Will you leave them here and let them roam?"
Mr. Rush smiled at her tender face,
admiring her charm and caring grace.
He could see she was brave with a loving heart.
So, he told her the plan that was soon to start.
"I will share with you an exciting mystery,
of how these animals will soon make history.
A journey across the countryside's best,
you and the bison on a train ride west."
They rounded up the bison, causing quite a show,
taking a herd of fifteen to the train depot.
Many people gathered to observe the display,
as workers loaded the train with water and hay.
They corralled the bison in crates so sturdy,
ensuring their comfort for the long journey.
The conductor waved, and the train was ready.
While the whistle blew, the bison stood steady.
The engine bellowed with clouds of thick steam.
Her very first train ride felt like a dream.
With her home far behind, there was no going back,
as the train rumbled faster down the westward track.
They traveled for miles watching everything in sight.
The trip was an adventure and quite a delight.
Huge crowds of people waved at each town.
Their faces of joy lifted her frown.
Their trip was long aboard the train so fast,
as she wondered how the bison would even last.
The impressive creatures stood strong and true,

Finding Refuge

waiting for the future as if they knew.
Days had passed before the last whistle blew.
Their final stop was finally in view.
The little town of Cache was straight ahead.
With horse and wagon, they would then be led.
Cowboys, ranchers, and folks from afar,
came to see them unload each railcar.
The crowd stared in awe as they opened the side door,
for many had never seen a big bison before.
The wagons were loaded and ready to go.
The last part of the trip would be very slow.
The horses kept pace, taking great care.
For everyone knew they were almost there.
Ample food and water and ready from rest,
the bison were anxious to finish the quest.
Numerous people gathered, their kindness to serve
a very warm welcome to the Wichita Game Preserve.
The woman observed with a curious gaze,
while several Indians began to amaze.
Proud tribal people, majestic and stern,
watched the historic scene of the buffalo's return.
As the buffalo neared, people began to rejoice.
Their cheerfulness and tears united in one voice.
"Why are they crying?" she walked up to ask.
"Bringing the bison here was such a great task!"
A Comanche girl shouted, "What a great day!
It's because the buffalo are here to stay.
Our tears are in answer to our hope and plea,
that once again the buffalo would roam free."
"Long ago, my ancestors used spear and knife.
To hunt the buffalo was their way of life.
These animals remind us of our cherished past.

Our wait to see them is over at last."
"You say they are 'buffalo' but how can that be?
Calling them that is very different to me."
"Some people say 'bison' is their given name.
But for us, they are 'buffalo' all the same."
The woman watched the celebration begin
and joined the nice girl and made a new friend.
Mr. Rush stopped and whispered in her ear,
"This is why all the buffalo are here."
She smiled at the excitement and could not wait,
as the buffalo charged through the open gate.
She watched the hot autumn sun sinking fast
and looked upon the land so wild and vast.
The Wichita Mountains stretched far and wide,
with grass-covered prairies rolling miles beside.
The magnificence of the preserve displayed great measure,
as she began to realize its beauty and treasure.
That happy October day of 1907,
Had become a moment as if from heaven.
A welcome place for the buffalo to live,
a place with more than her home could give.
The people expressed their joy and pride.
As the woman saw, it was worth the ride.
The grateful girl reached out for her hand
and pointed west with an arching span.
A vast domain of plains and heat,
of sweeping wind and waving wheat.
"Oklahoma is their land and home,
for this is where the mighty roam."

Milton Keynes UK
Ingram Content Group UK Ltd.
UKHW041005111124
451035UK00002B/348